The Penny Detective

John Tallon Jones

Published by G-L-R (Great Little Read)

CONTENTS

CHAPTER ONE..4

CHAPTER TWO..11

CHAPTER THREE 18

CHAPTER FOUR 24

CHAPTER FIVE 28

CHAPTER SIX..32

CHAPTER SEVEN 37

CHAPTER EIGHT 43

CHAPTER NINE 46

CHAPTER TEN 51

CHAPTER ELEVEN 57

CHAPTER TWELVE...64

CHAPTER THIRTEEN 68

CHAPTER FOURTEEN 78

CHAPTER FIFTEEN 89

CHAPTER SIXTEEN 96

CHAPTER SEVENTEEN 102

CHAPTER EIGHTEEN 115

CHAPTER NINETEEN 119

CHAPTER TWENTY 122

CHAPTER TWENTY-ONE...126

CHAPTER TWENTY-TWO...134

EPILOGUE..142

WINTER 1985

CHAPTER ONE

I was christened Stanley Morris-Shannon, but only my mum calls me Stanley, and only then when she is ticked off with me. Most other people, including my dad, call me Morris or Moggsy. I'm a private detective and got into the business by doing what most people do if they are desperate to get a job; I went on a course. The course lasted for a whole four weeks, and the main reason that persuaded me to part with my dad's money to go on it was that I could do most of the studying from home, in between watching afternoon chat shows on TV. The company used a technique that it called distance learning and what I called a rip-off.

I guess I'm an okay kind of fella though I don't have that many friends. I live in a block of council flats, which suits me down to the ground, though my mum and dad keep telling me that at thirty I should have done better for myself and be married with a couple of kids, and doing a job with regular hours. The fact that dad retired and they moved to the Costa del Sol means that I get less earache. The fact that dad is also a multi-millionaire helps as well because on the allowance he set up for me, I'm not well off, but comfortable enough not to have to do a poxy office job.

I've spent a lot of time living rough in my life, trying to rebel against my public school education, and the family plan to tame the animal inside me enough to carry on the family business. In the end, the life I was leading got too much for even me, and so now, I've given up on the road, and dad has given up trying to change me and sold his used car business. It was mum that made him move to Spain, and it was her that persuaded him to give me an allowance that was not enough for me to kill myself with fast cars and hookers, but sufficient to keep me off the social and pay the rent for my one-bedroom bachelor pad.

As a result of an investigation, I was hospitalised last week with suspected concussion and severely bruised ribs; but to be honest, for the most part, my job is nothing out of the ordinary, and can often be quite boring and tedious. This was the first time that I had ever been injured while working, but it was my own fault, really. I had been hired to trace a runaway and tracked her down to some waste ground behind the Westhill Housing Estate at the back of the town centre. I thought that I had caught her, but she was a fast runner and agile too because the way she climbed that tree and sat there at the top looking down and daring me to follow, took some guts.

I don't have a head for heights, and for the money I was getting paid, I should have turned around and gone home. For all of the thanks I got for my trouble off the client, I wish I had. I like to see a job through though, so I climbed up, and when I was close enough made a grab for her. She scratched me, but I managed to hold on as we both fell backwards. I ended up severely concussed and wracked with pain on the floor under the tree. Fluffy sat on my chest, licking herself and purring for a couple of seconds, before disappearing into the distance and eventually making her way home.

Most of the jobs I am hired to do aren't as exciting as that one or as dangerous, but from time to time something vaguely interesting happens, and this was the case last week when Karl Ashford dropped by my office. My place of work is not what you would call plush, but the shabbiness has a kind of unique charm that I like and which suits the clientele that pay for my services. I occupy a room above a betting shop on the High Street in Croxley Greater Merseyside. I have an answerphone to pick up my calls when I'm out and to keep the outgoings to a minimum I do my own cleaning and my own accounts.

I was doing the cleaning when Karl walked in on me, and though I had never met him before, I knew of him and his brother and had a pretty good idea what he had come to see me about.

Both Karl and his brother Billy were minor league villains and, for the most part, contented themselves with dealing in a bit of weed, and some petty thieving. Unfortunately, brother, Billy had just got promoted to the First Division and was now on the most-wanted list of the Merseyside Constabulary for murdering his wife's ex-lover, local businessman, Tony O'Brian.

Karl was probably in his late forties, but his lack of hair and grey stubbly pockmarked features made him look a lot older. You got the impression when you were in the same room as him that you were only a couple of words away from getting your head kicked in, but between the two brothers, it was Billy who most locals steered clear of as he had a reputation as a nasty piece of shit. Younger brother Karl, even though he looked like a gorilla was technically the brains behind the muscle, and rarely resorted to violence. Get on the wrong side of an Ashford however, and you would eventually end up severely injured. Go to bed with the wife of an Ashford, and you more than likely would end up like Tony O'Brian.

I was a bit surprised to see him standing by the door when I turned off the cleaner, and how long he had been there, I couldn't say. The truth is, I would have been surprised to see anyone at that moment as work had been a bit slack, to say the least, and apart from my mate Shoddy dropping by to borrow money to fund his drinking habit, he was the first person to come into the office for a week.

"Are you, Morris Shannon?" He asked, looking at the cleaner, then letting his eyes drift around the room. He had the sort of face that didn't give much away about what he was thinking.

"That's me. What can I do for you?" I made a vague hand gesture for him to take a seat.

He sat down and waited for me to wind the lead in, put the vacuum cleaner away in the cupboard and sit down behind my desk.

"You know who I am?" He asked.

"I know about what happened to your brother if that's what you mean."

"Ok then, so I'll cut out the shit and get to the point. Billy didn't have anything to do with killing O'Brian, and I know that for a fact."

"If you're so sure, then why not go to the police, and save them the trouble of looking for Billy?"

He shook his head and smiled coldly. "I wish it was that simple, Mr Shannon, but what I'm going to tell you is between you and me, and can't go no further." He looked at me before continuing, and I nodded.

"Billy couldn't have set the fire that night because he was robbing a warehouse in Bootle with me."

I repeated my original question. "So, what can I do for you?"

"I want you to find out who did kill him and let me know."

I didn't say anything, hoping that he would fill in the silence with some details that I didn't already know, and was relieved when he obliged.

"The police just want a conviction, and they don't give a damn if it's the right one. Billy is the easy target, and his alibi is a pile of shit, which would put us both away, so you can appreciate the predicament we're in."

"Who do you think killed him?"

"Take your pick; O'Brian was a flash bastard and was no boy scout when it came to making money. There were a few people around here that were happy when he ended up like a roast chicken."

"Including Billy?"

"Billy wasn't bothered either way; he and Clair had what you might call an open marriage, and Billy knew the score and was no angel himself when it came to shacking up with women behind Clair's back. The whole business between O'Brian and Clair happened years ago, so why would Billy do something about it now? Why wait when he could have dealt with it at the time?"

"Where is Billy now?"

"Your guess is as good as mine; he's done a runner, and didn't tell me where he was going. I wish that I knew myself, but that's not important. What is important is to find the bloke that did it so that we can get Billy out of the shit."

"Why choose me, there are bigger agencies in Liverpool?"

Karl shrugged. "Are you telling me you don't need the business?" He looked around the office again and then fixed me with a pair of ice grey eyes.

I needed the business alright; my car needed a service, and the road tax was due. I shoved a form in his general direction as fast as I could, while maintaining steady eye contact.

He filled in his details, then threw a brown envelope at me. "Here are some names of people that you could try for starters and some cash for expenses."

He stood up; we shook hands, and I told him that I would do some work and get back to him when I had something to report. He seemed satisfied by that and let himself out.

CHAPTER TWO

Croxley is not one of the classiest areas on Merseyside; in fact, I would go so far as to say that it is a shit-hole. Just a collection of streets shaded in with damp red brick buildings that have dirty windows and ugly high-rise flats, with a sprinkling of parks, shops, pubs, clubs and Catholic Churches. All street corners come complete with obligatory gangs of jobless scallies, and all roads lead to the M6, and possibly onwards to the M1 and London if you're brave enough. But if you hadn't realised it already, the main drag will take you through the town's boarded up, decaying shopping centre that gives you a definite feeling that life here is at the sharp end of destitution. The only good thing they say to come out of Croxley is the road to the Wirral.

Still; looking on the bright side, there are so many scams, robberies and muggings going on around town that the real police can't cope, and they have given up trying, so there is plenty of work for a good private detective, which I wish I was. You could say that I am in the right place at the right time with the wrong skills. Before Karl had walked through my door and thrown money at me, I was thinking of jacking it in, getting another loan from my dad and opening a fish and chip shop.

I left the office a couple of minutes after Karl, having waited with my coat on to give him time to clear the stairs. As I walked along the High Street, I racked my brains for what I knew about the murder of O'Brian. Funnily enough, I used to work for him a few years ago, as a doorman in one of his clubs. Back then, I had long hair and just about got away with this line of work without serious injury because I am six feet four. This tended to put the drunks off having a pop at me, but people told me that my face was just too sweet looking to be a proper bouncer. It was during my time working for O'Brian that I had a brainwave. I shaved my hair off and developed a menacing leer. This seemed to do the trick with most punters. In those days, I was the master of the vice-like grip around the top of the arm, and a quiet word if trouble started. This usually meant I kept my tuxedo a blood-free zone, which saved on the dry cleaning bills. I never did grow my hair back, and I'm still developing variations of that menacing sneer.

I never met O'Brian to speak to but didn't need a one on one with him to realise what he was about. I always put his aggressive streak down to the fact that he was very small with red hair. Even when I was working for him, he was known as a bit of a bad lad who didn't mind getting rough if he couldn't do it the friendly way. He'd managed to get a fair size business together, with a couple of clubs, some betting shops, and flats that he rented out to students and low-life. There were always rumours about the man flying around the streets, especially about how he had started off his empire by running a protection racket. Businesses in the area would pay him money every month to avoid getting their premises burnt. It smacked a little bit of ironic justice to me, seeing how he had died with his hands tied behind his back in a fire.

Whoever had killed him and for whatever reason, I doubted that there would be many tears shed for the guy. At fifty-five, with at least twelve years of making enemies in Croxley alone, the Sharks would already be assembling ready to divide up his business interests, many of which were now totally legit.

The night he died, from what I could remember from the local newspaper, he was last seen at around midnight in one of his clubs called the Oasis. He'd got a phone call and left in a hurry, and then neighbours reported smoke and flames coming out of his house at around four in the morning. By the time the fire brigade lads could get inside, all that remained of the poor bastard was charcoal, but it was later found out that his hands had been tied, and his head smashed in with something akin to a sledgehammer.

The reason Billy's name came up so quickly was because of information given to the police from an anonymous source. The reason Billy managed to escape out of the back door of his house was that the police arrived with sirens blazing in the early hours of the morning. They could just as easily have sent him a letter asking if he could be in when they called. I guessed that the chief inspector who had cocked this one up was getting some earache off his boss and was probably back on traffic duty.

This all happened about a month ago, and Billy has not been seen since. The press picked up the story of Billy's wife, Clair, being the ex-lover of O'Brian, again, through an anonymous call, though the police didn't confirm or deny it officially. That's the crappy thing about living in Croxley. Everybody wants to know your business, and there is very little you can get away with without someone finding out and passing it around. The only people that didn't seem to have a clue about what was going on in Croxley were the police. The official reason for Billy being number one suspect had not been released, though the fact that he ran away didn't look good.

My flat is on the second floor of a high-rise complex that was condemned as unfit for human habitation twenty years ago and is only a twenty-minute walk from my office. The lift very rarely works, and when it does it gives you the impression that it won't be working for long. You feel grateful when the doors eventually open, and you are free to leave and carry on your life. The two-floor climb I write off as my daily workout, and today I did the stairs two at a time, before arriving wheezing and red-faced at the door of my next-door neighbour and best friend, Shoddy.

The figure that opened the door and let me in was a curious mix to look at. To someone that didn't know him, Shoddy would more than likely be written off as a bum. I could smell the cider in the air as he led me through to his combined lounge and kitchen. I sat down,and he cleared a couple of empty cans of Special Brew into the waste paper basket and poured me a glass of cheap Bulgarian cider.

Shoddy is in his late forties with a face that has a derelict aura. There are bags under the bags of his washed-out blue eyes, and his grey receding hairline and lack of teeth is finished off nicely by nicotine-stained fingers and a permanent odour of ready- rubbed tobacco and cheap booze.

The man looked as if he belonged in a shop doorway sleeping under a pile of newspapers, and sometimes it was hard even for me to believe that when I first met him he was a top-cop that was on his way to a position in the higher echelons of the Liverpool Police Force. Drink and heroin addiction stopped all that, and he was relieved of his post on the grounds of ill health, after trying to kill himself with Paraquat. The pressure had somehow got to him, and he had never told me the reason it all turned bad, but it must have been something pretty heavy.

These days the bags of heroin are a distant memory, and he contents himself with blocking out reality with strong cider for breakfast and cheap cans of supermarket lager. But you would be a fool to think that Shoddy was a vegetable even though he often smelt like one. He had the sharpest mind of anyone I have ever known, and still had some good police contacts, who remembered what he once had been. For me, he was the ideal person to do all of the boring detail work that was a big part of being a private detective, and the best part of our working relationship was that he worked for tobacco and booze.

I sat in an old armchair, and he settled on the settee across from me and started rolling a cigarette. "What's up, Moggsy? You're not usually home this early."

"What would you say if I told you I got a visit from Karl Ashford a bit ago, and he gave me money to prove that brother Billy was innocent?"

That certainly stopped him rolling; well, only for a couple of seconds. As he picked a bit of tobacco out of his cigarette and put it in his tin; without looking at me, he said, "I hope you threw it back at him and told him where to go."

"Work is work, mate, and we haven't had too much lately."

He lit his cigarette, shook his head, and spit out a piece of tobacco. "It's cut and dried as far as I can see. He was caught shagging an Ashford, and they killed him. That's what they do. It smells of trouble to me, and I think you'd be an idiot to get involved. Let the police sort it out. Even they can't make a hash of this one, and it's just a matter of time before they get him."

"We shook hands. I've already agreed to take the case."

He shrugged. "So what's the deal, Moggs?"

"He gave me some names for starters, but what I want is some more background information on O'Brian. Dig around and see if he has upset anybody recently, or find out who would have benefitted from him being dead."

I knew from the look on his face that he thought I wanted my head examining, and probably also thought like I did that I was out of my depth on this one. But if there was one thing that you could count on with Shoddy, it was that he would go along with you, even if he didn't agree with what you were doing.

"I'll poke a few contacts with my stick and see what comes up, but it's gonna cost. How much did he give you?"

CHAPTER THREE

My local is a pub called the Old One Hundred, which is just around the corner from my flat. It's not one of those trendy city bars that seem to be springing up everywhere these days; it's the kind of place you can get seriously drunk, in the company of serious drunks. Shoddy has his own pewter tankard that the landlord, Bill, keeps behind the bar for him, and I have my favourite seat in the snug. This is a little room off the main bar area, with a scattering of rough-looking, heavy duty green, leather armchairs and some tables, which could give you some severe splinters if you didn't treat them with respect. Around the walls, there are pictures of soldiers from the First World War, which must be some significant factor on how the pub got its name, but nobody I have ever spoken to knows what the connection is.

The Hundred hasn't seen a lick of paint in my lifetime, and the violent vibe at closing time is the main reason students, and trendies stay well clear. They prefer the new wine bar across the street, or a bus into Liverpool. I love the pub because the beer is cheap, the decor doesn't make you feel out of place, and it's just a short stagger home.

I was here having a couple of beers and looking through the information that Karl had given me, which, to say the least, was scant. Apart from his telephone number, there were several names listed. Six of them were employees from O'Brian's business interests, but the one at the top was his business partner. This was a guy I didn't know called Steve Carney. I have to admit I was surprised that Clair Ashford hadn't made the top ten, but I had already added her that morning, and given her a call. She had agreed to meet me though didn't want me around her house, so was due to arrive any minute. Another surprise; either she didn't know how down market The Hundred was, or she was a serious drinker and didn't care. I was waiting with bated breath to find out when she walked in.

The way that she had hesitated at the door and nearly walked out again told me all I wanted to know. You don't get any women coming into establishments like The Hundred on their own. Not even hookers would chance it, so I knew it was her immediately. The fact that I was in the snug gave me the time to look her over: me, and most of the other men in the room. She was a bottle blonde around fifty, and a bit overweight. She was too big-boned for my taste but still a sexy woman. I don't know much about clothes but know class when I see it, and she oozed it as she walked toward the bar. I intercepted her and directed her to my table before she reached landlord Bill. He was waiting by the bar with hungry eyes, drying a half-pint glass, with his tongue hanging out. She slid into the chair across from mine and eased herself provocatively out of her fake-fur coat.

I bought her a gin and tonic and filled her in on the reason I wanted to talk to her. She didn't look surprised. It was as if Karl had already mentioned me to her.

Whether she was in mourning for her ex-lover or worried about where Billy was, she didn't say. In fact, I didn't pick up any signals about the mood she was in, but she was obviously not dancing on air to be sitting with me.

"What time did Billy get home that night?"

She shrugged and shook her head. "I couldn't say because I was asleep. I know he was in bed when the police arrived and couldn't get out of the house quick enough."

I wished that I had written down a few questions because my brain was blank and wasn't sending any through to my mouth. "Do you think that Billy killed him?" I blurted out.

"Of course I don't, you daft bugger. Whatever Billy was he wasn't a killer, and didn't Karl tell you what he was doing that night?" She lowered her voice. "They were knocking off some warehouse out in Bootle, and that's why he got out of the house so quickly when the police arrived. He thought it was about that, and so did I at the time."

"How come he hasn't been in touch?"

"That depends."

"On what?"

"On who he is shacking up with. Billy is not a killer, but he is a lying, cheating womaniser, and I've not got the slightest doubt that he is with one of them now. He collects women like some people collect stamps. It's his hobby. I've put up with it for years, and I know that he's never going to change."

"And you and Tony O'Brian? Didn't you have a little bit of a thing for each other?"

She glared at me. "You've been reading the newspapers I see, Luv. So I had a bit of a fling with Tony. So what? Sometimes I get so pissed-off with Billy that I try to get him jealous, but it's like water off a duck's back. He knows I love him, and he takes advantage."

"What's the story with O'Brian, Clair? How serious did it get?"

"A couple of years ago, I used to work in one of Tony's betting shops. We got friendly, had a few drinks after work, and he took me out for a couple of meals. At the time, Billy was living with some slut in North Wales, so he couldn't say much about who I went to bed with, but it never got that far. Tony always treated me okay. He was more of a shoulder to cry on, and I certainly needed that at the time. When Billy came back, I gave up the job and didn't see much of him again. Billy never said anything about it, so it's just water under the bridge."

"Are you sure he didn't hold a grudge against O'Brian?"

Clair shrugged, "As sure as I can be. I can't ask him at the moment, can I? How do I know what's in his head? If you want my opinion, there are people around here with bigger motives for killing Tony than my Billy."

"Karl said Billy hasn't been in touch with him either."

"If he is with one of his girlfriends, then he's not going to. Karl has given him a few beatings, over the trouble he's caused me, and he's not going to be too pleased if he's up to his old tricks."

"Who do you think killed O'Brian?"

"Look, Shannon, I don't know, and I don't bloody care. All that I do know is that my Billy didn't. You're the detective, so do some detecting. You could start by looking at the people he worked with. That partner of his is doing okay now Tony is out of the way, why not try him?"

I intend to, and a few other as well. When was the last time that you saw O'Brian?"

"Not for a while. Probably about six months. The last time that I saw him was on that TV programme about drugs being sold to the kids in Liverpool. He was only on it briefly, and I could see that he wasn't too pleased. He almost hit the reporter that tried to interview him about drug dealing in his clubs, but that was Tony. He had a knack for getting on the wrong side of people, and if you want my opinion, he must have upset the wrong person."

I finished off my beer and walked her to the car park. Her car was parked near to the front door. It was a white Ford Capri with a red

Starsky and Hutch racing stripe down both sides. I watched as she drove away and walked back to my flat.

When I got home, I made myself a sandwich, pulled a bottle of beer from the fridge and went out on the balcony. It creaked as I sat down on an old deck chair, and as always I wondered if it was going to hold my weight, or collapse and sending me tumbling into the night. I watched the lights of cars on the motorway in the distance and listened to their soothing low rumble while I munched on cheese and pickle and drank a light ale. I made a mental note to write down some proper questions for O'Brian's partner Steve Carney and hoped that Shoddy had stayed sober long enough to do some research.

By eleven o'clock, I was in bed and sleeping like a baby.

CHAPTER FOUR

I got into my office early the next morning to do some creative accounting with the money that Karl Ashford had given me, and try to get an appointment with Carney. He was a difficult man to track down, and when I did eventually talk to him, he wasn't too keen to meet-up. He eventually grudgingly agreed to give me five minutes later on that day at his office. The office he was using was a backroom in one of the clubs that he and O'Brian jointly owned called the Oasis, which was situated on the Milbank Estate.

By lunchtime, I had decided how much of the cash I was going to put through the accounts and how much went in my back pocket. I gave Shoddy a ring to get some background on Carney and to see how he was getting on. He was on his way out but was upbeat about what he had done so far, and we arranged to meet at his place later. Off the top of his head, he told me that Carney didn't have a criminal record, which could either mean that he was straight or very clever. He had worked a couple of years for O'Brian before being made a partner in the business.

I left the office, fired up my Riley Elf and headed for the motorway. The Elf is a bit classier than a Mini but possibly a curious choice of car for someone my size. I bought it because it was cheap and easy enough to maintain so that I could do the servicing myself. The fact that it was difficult for me to get in and out, and that my head was constantly hitting the roof as I drove were side-issues that I never liked to discuss.

The drive to the Oasis didn't take that long, and when I arrived, the only other car in the car park was a Jaguar. I parked the Elf as close as I could to it, safe in the knowledge that if I were a thief I knew which one I'd choose.

The building was a nondescript rectangle of red brick with no visible windows and looked like a factory, which is what it probably had been once. The thick black metal-backed door was ajar, and I pushed my way into a small reception area complete with till and counter with empty coat hanger racks at the back. There was a black curtain covering an entrance. This took me through into the main room, which had a bar the length of one wall and a small circular dance floor with banks of lights above it. The place smelt like Shoddy's flat, with a slight underlying aroma of sweat, cheap perfume and aftershave.

There were tables and chairs around the dance area and stairs that led up to a balcony, which circled the top of the room. Above the balcony, the deejay equipment was situated in a little glass booth that was only accessible by a short ladder. Steve Carney was nowhere to be seen, so I pushed on through a door marked private. At the end of a dim corridor I came to a door marked office and knocked.

The person that greeted me when I walked in was not what I expected. He was bald on top and had the face of an accountant rather than a club owner. I put his age at somewhere in his fifties, but the John Lennon glasses and pinstripe suit made it difficult to put a definite handle on him. He was bent over a large green ledger with lots of numbers and names in it. He looked up at me with the face of a man that was not impressed that he had been disturbed, but was too timid to say anything about it. He pushed the ledger to one side, took his glasses off and rubbed his eyes.

"You must be, Mr Shannon." He looked at his watch. "You're on time to the minute. I'm impressed." He put his glasses back on, and his voice became more businesslike and unfriendly. "What can I do for you? I can give you a couple of minutes, and then I have to lock up."

"I've been asked to look into the death of Tony O'Brian, and talking to you was an obvious first step."

He gestured for me to take a seat, and did the tired eyes trick again. "Who are you working for, Mr Shannon, or are you going to let me guess?"

"It's no secret; I'm being paid by the Ashford family."

This made him smile, and he suddenly became interested in the ledger that he had been reading when I came in. He didn't look at me when he spoke but started writing. "I heard that Karl was a bit confused about his brother's part in Tony's murder, but you would expect that from his sort."

"And what sort is that?"

"Well, it's not for me to say, as you are on his payroll, and I don't want to end up like Tony. The police seem to think that it is pretty much cut and dried, and that's good enough for me. I think that you are wasting your time looking for another angle. Running away didn't do much for Mr Ashford's defence either."

"Can you think of anybody else that could have been upset by Tony O'Brian?"

"I could give you a list if I had the time." He looked at his watch again. "Which I haven't, so if you don't mind, I am going to have to lock up."

He got up and walked me through the club. I had one last throw before he closed the door in my face. "Would you mind if I came back and talked to some of the staff?"

He held the door open for me and waited for me to walk out before he answered. "If you must, Mr Shannon, but remember they are here to work so come early, and you are going to have to pay to get in like everybody else."

He had closed the door before I had a chance to say anything else.

CHAPTER FIVE

Shoddy had surpassed my limited expectations of him when we met up in his flat later that afternoon. In the lounge, he had rigged up an easel and had written down the relevant names that we had got so far, so we could look where they all fitted in with each other. I didn't know where he got all his information from, as the four-week course on detecting didn't do much more than show you the basics, and I never bothered reading any of it anyway. Shoddy was worth his weight in tobacco.

While he was cooking cheese on toast with fried eggs and beans for our dinner, I scanned his notes for clues. O'Brian had only moved to Croxley about twelve years ago, and for any information before that, Shoddy had written pending, in red. What he had been up to in the area since arriving was easier to trace. He had bought two nightclubs, the Oasis and the Kabin. The previous owners had decided suddenly to get out of the nightclub trade and leave the area.

After acquiring the clubs, he bought a couple of betting shops and lots of flats that he rented out mainly to students and low-income families. There was talk that he had a money-lending racket and also leaned on local businesses around Croxley for protection money. Nothing was ever proven, and the police never seemed interested in doing any investigating. This led a lot of people in the know to acknowledge that he had some serious friends in high places. He had never been married, lived on his own, and was not known to be a womaniser or drug user. He had one conviction in his late teens for assault. Shoddy was waiting for more details on this.

Steve Carney looked like an accountant but was, in fact, a solicitor. He had been involved right from the start with O'Brian's acquisitions and was responsible for making sure that everything was done legally. There was never talk of any misdemeanour on his part, and the reason that he was made a partner seemed to be that almost all of his work was to do with O'Brian's business dealings. He probably knew so much about the man, that it was best to tie him in to make sure that he kept his mouth shut. Carney was not married and was rumoured to have a preference for young men, and dressing up like a schoolgirl.

Clair Jones was a local girl who became an Ashford at eighteen when she married childhood sweetheart Billy. Their marriage had not produced children, and the thirty or so years they had spent together could not be described as blissful. Clair had left on a few occasions, and Billy had an addictive womanising streak. It was rumoured that he beat her up frequently and at one time had been hospitalised because of her injuries. The police were never involved, as she never pressed charges.

There was no information about any of O'Brian's staff, so I assumed that this was pending too.

"What do you think?" Shoddy pushed a plate into my hand and gave me a knife and fork.

"Where did you get all of the info, and when will you sort out the pending?"

"That's just information gathered here and there from people I know. The other stuff will take me a bit of time and needs a lot of legwork, and a peek at some police records."

Shoddy began forking pieces of toast into his mouth with the ferocity of someone who hasn't eaten for a while. "I still think you're wasting your time on this, Moggsy. Everybody I've talked to thinks it was Billy. The only variation on that theory is that it was him and his brother, which is also a possibility. I haven't got round to talking to any of the police lads down the station, but they're not that creative mentally when it comes to crime. They just go for the solution that is easy and gives them less paperwork, so they can get to the pub quicker."

"Carney says that O'Brian had a load of enemies. Why not one of them?"

Shoddy pushed his plate away and burped. "Let's see what I can find out before jumping to any conclusion. You've got to learn to have more of an open mind, Moggsy, if you're gonna make a good private investigator." He got up and walked to his easel. "What we have got so far is the charred body of a man and a suspect with a motive. That suspect has disappeared, which doesn't give his defence many marks out of ten for credibility. Did you ask Carney what he was doing on the night of the fire?"

I shook my head. "I'm sorry, it slipped my mind."

"That's okay; I will see if I can find it in the police files as they certainly would have interviewed him and looked at his alibi very carefully."

I remembered what Clair had told me about the television programme. "Did you run across any mention of a TV programme O'Brian was in about drugs being sold in his clubs?"

"I didn't hear anything about that, but it's worth a look, what was it called?"

"That's all I know, but it shouldn't take a man of your professionalism long to track it down."

"Okay, I'll put it on the list. That's me sorted out for the next couple of days, what are you up to, Moggs?"

I looked at my watch. "Well, I'm going clubbing in a bit to see if I can get anything from some of the names on the list Karl Ashford gave me. Somebody must at least have an opinion on who killed O'Brian, so I might get lucky."

Don't hold your breath, Moggsy, and be very careful. If Billy didn't do it the person who did might want to stop you asking questions permanently."

CHAPTER SIX

I arrived at the Oasis club at around half-past ten without much of a plan about what I was going to do when I got inside. However, if I had got to pay for the privilege I was determined that it wasn't going to be a wasted trip.

The place was not busy and wouldn't be until the pubs closed at eleven o'clock. Only losers, dance freaks, and Motown music lovers ever got to a club this early, and there was more staff than punters, which suited my purpose. I ordered a whisky and coke and drew my first blank from the waitress behind the bar, who said that this was her first night and that she didn't know anything about O'Brian. I was going to end up seriously drunk if I had to go through all of the bar staff to get any information, so I asked her to point out Teresa Savage, who didn't work there anymore, Alice Stewart, who was off sick, and Colin Dicks, who she had never heard of.

It wasn't looking too good, and the music was beginning to annoy me, but the entrance fee made me stay. I was on my third whisky and coke, and getting the eye from a girl sitting on a barstool a few feet away when an arm grabbed me around the throat from behind.

"Make one move, and I'm going to break your neck."

I instinctively grabbed the arm and tried to loosen the grip, but it was rock hard. I felt the pressure release for a split second and jumped off the stool sending it flying. I turned around at the same time and got ready to kick whoever it was in the balls.

"You're losing your touch, Moggsy. Ten years ago, and I would have been on my way to the hospital by now."

I dropped my guard and straightened my tie. "Nice move, Eddie. You must have just had your yearly bath because I usually would have smelt you before you had a chance to get that close."

Eddie held out his hand and laughed. I took it, and he put his arm around my shoulders and patted my back like I was a dog. There were not many people I have ever met that I could look in the eyes without having to bend my legs, but Eddie Seer was one of them. He was a beast of a man and built like a Chieftain Tank, but usually as gentle as a baby unless he was provoked. I hadn't seen him since we worked the doors together, at least ten years ago. Even though he was thinner on top, he looked in excellent shape. Apart from being a great guy, Eddie was the toughest man I have ever met, and, believe me, I have met a lot who thought they were tough but just liked boasting.

"The last I heard of you, mate, was that you had joined the army. What happened, Ed?"

"Did my time is what happened. I could have signed on for more, but with all the Irish business going on it's safer as a civilian."

"Can I buy you a drink?"

"No thanks, Moggsy, I'm working."

"How long have you been working here?"

"I started a couple of months ago. Do you remember we used to work for Tony O'Brian in the old days? Well, he gave me my old job back. Did you hear that he got fried?"

"Funny you should say that, but it's the reason I'm here tonight." I filled him in on the details, and when I finished, he let out a whistle.

"Who do you suspect beside Billy Ashford?"

"Too early to say yet, but I guess just because his wife and Karl think he is innocent, it doesn't mean that he is. I would like to know where Billy is right now, so I could at least hear what his side of the story is."

"How did you get into the detective business? I always thought you would give in to your dad and be living the high life of Mercedes and call girls. How is the old man?"

"He gave up trying, and they retired to Spain. Detecting ain't so bad, though the hours are a bit shit."

"I hope you're charging the Ashfords time and a half for tonight."

I laughed. "What's your view of the events? Did anything happen in the club before he was killed?"

Eddie rubbed his chin. "Nothing cut and dried like a death threat letter or stuff like that. Maybe O'Brian had a butler you could blame it on, or it could have been his partner, Carney."

I ordered another whiskey and coke. "Did Carney have anything to gain from getting rid of O'Brian?"

Eddie thought for a minute and shook his head. "I heard that he was pretty rich already and was doing alright, but you never can tell. If you ask me, he isn't a killer, and I heard that O'Brian had been beaten with a hammer, which smacks of someone very angry. Carney is too much of a wimp for that type of thing, though I suppose he could have paid someone."

"Like Billy Ashford?"

"I've never met the guy, but you tell me? Was he the sort of bloke that would do that to someone's skull?"

"Who knows, Eddie? That's what I am being paid to find out." I finished off my whisky and held out my hand. He took it and did the dog pat on my back again. I guess he was just really pleased to see me. He walked me to the door, and I gave him my telephone numbers and office address. I told him not to be a stranger and meant it. He followed me to my car.

"There is something, now I come to think of it, that I thought was a bit strange, but it may be nothing. A girl called Teresa Savage who worked the bar was very chummy with O'Brian. There was something not quite right, but I couldn't put my finger on what it was. It might just be me imagining things after what happened."

"How do you mean?"

"Well, for a start, she must have been in her late forties, and all the other girls are in their twenties and very pretty. You know the score with staff in clubs, Moggsy. They are like a little family and nothing gets missed. The rumour was they were having an affair. She spent too much time in his office, and once or twice he took her home at the end of the night. She was only here for six months, not much longer than me, and he made her a supervisor. After that, she was a right bitch with the bar staff, and everybody hated her guts."

"What happened to her?"

" After the night he got burnt nobody has seen her. She just left. Now, if I were investigating this, I would check out where she is, and what she has got to say for herself."

CHAPTER SEVEN

It was a couple of days before Shoddy had got enough together to set up a meeting, and in this time I contented myself watching afternoon television and hanging around The Hundred. I felt a bit guilty spending Karl's money on beer and fast food, especially as I had not dug anything up to help Billy. A big part of being a private detective is really tedious work, and luckily I had Shoddy who had the kind of brain that enjoyed that sort of thing. We were the perfect team, but more like Laurel and Hardy than Holmes and Watson.

When I got to Shoddy's, he looked tired, and a bit unsteady on his feet, and that gave me even more of a pang of guilt. The gleam in his eye and the new information on the easel told me that his digging had turned up something, and I sat down and waited to be informed of developments. It almost gave me a feeling of professionalism; until Shoddy handed me a cheese and tomato toasty and a can of cider, then passed out on the settee. I realised that the gleam in his eye was just a sign that he had drunk too much Carlsberg Special Brew. On an up-note, the hour or so that it took for him to come round, gave me ample time to go through his notes, which due to his police training were immaculate.

Everything that we had discussed had been dealt with and most of the items marked 'pending' before, were now brimming with information.

There had been a warehouse broken into in Bootle on the night that O'Brian had died, but according to evidence given by a night watchman who had been tied up by a gang of four masked men; it was all over by around midnight. This would have given Billy plenty of time to get back to Croxley and commit the murder.

O'Brian had been convicted of assault and given a twelve-month suspended sentence in Belfast when he was nineteen. The person that he assaulted was a man called Ralph Carroll, who was a factory manager.

The assault only carried a suspended sentence because it was in self-defence though O'Brian had been thought to have used undue force. He had had put Mr Carroll into intensive care. Carroll had been angry because O'Brian had been dating his sixteen-year-old daughter and had got her pregnant. There was talk about a case for statutory rape, but because it was too difficult to prove it was not pursued. Shoddy had even got an address for Julie Carroll, who was now living in Dewsbury and had never married.

There was still a big 'pending' against the names of the employees that Karl had given me, though partner Steve Carney had got an alibi for the night in question. A college student named David Davies, who said that he had been with him all night, and had left the next morning at 9 o'clock.

The television show that Clair Ashford was talking about was a one-hour special screened around two months before O'Brian's death. It dealt with the subject of drugs being sold to young people in clubs in the area. On the show, O'Brian had appeared for less than twenty seconds and flew into a rage on camera with the investigative journalist who was trying to ask him questions about the sale of heroin on his premises. The reporter's microphone had been knocked from his hand by O' Brian who had to be restrained by colleagues.

On Billy Ashford, there was nothing. The police had drawn a complete blank, and there had been some very red faces about the sirens. Police did not link Billy or Karl to the Warehouse job in Bootle, and Shoddy had not given them any reason to do so.

There was nothing in his report about the police interviewing Teresa Savage though I did read through statements from a lot of the other staff, who didn't say very much. There was nothing that I read, which was substantial enough to think it was anyone other than Billy Ashford who was the killer.

When Shoddy eventually was capable of speech it was around eleven o'clock. He made us both a cup of bedtime cocoa and stood up as best he could by his easel while I helped myself to chocolate digestive biscuits.

"I couldn't get any information on the people that worked for O'Brian, but the stuff about the conviction looks interesting and was difficult to get hold of." He took a swig of cocoa and frowned. "I still think Billy murdered him and so does everybody else. The warehouse robbery wasn't a very good alibi, and now it has been blown apart he hasn't got much else going for him."

I tried to think of an argument against Shoddy's reasoning but failed to come up with one. In the end, it was Shoddy himself that gave me something to keep the case alive.

"Julie Carroll, the girl that got pregnant by O'Brian, could be useful and may give you an insight into something, but I'm not sure if I know what it is. At least, you can claim expenses for going to Dewsbury."

"Do you think that she may have something to do with it?"

"It all happened a long time ago so I would be surprised, but what I always used to say when I was a detective constable was if there are no obvious leads then look at the un-obvious."

"So, do you think that this could throw up a couple of names?"

Shoddy shook his head. "You know what I think, Moggsy, but if you've taken the cash, then you should at least be seen to be doing some detecting. I would give Karl a call and let him know what you have been up to so far. You never know, he may give you some more money if he's desperate enough. Lay it on thick and say that you may be close to a breakthrough."

I told him what Eddie had mentioned in the club about the strange relationship O'Brian had with Teresa Savage, and he said she was also worth a visit. He promised to get me an address for when I came back from Dewsbury. I left around midnight and let myself into my flat, looking forward to my bed.

I knew that there was something wrong when I opened the door. Two cushions off the settee were blocking my way in, and I pushed them aside and entered. My flat had been trashed. I knocked on Shoddy's door and asked him to come and take a look, more for moral support than fear that anybody was still there.

"This puts a different angle on things," he said, picking up the drawers of a cabinet and sliding them back in. "I told you that you might have spooked someone, and it looks as though you have. Whether it is the killer remains to be seen."

"What do you think he was looking for here?"

"Looking for something or trying to scare you. Who knows? I would check out the office if I were you."

If this was an attempt to frighten me, it had worked. The thought that someone had been through my stuff felt a bit freaky.

After saying goodnight again to Shoddy, I piled furniture up against the door and placed a tray of glasses on top.

If anybody tried to get in tonight, I was going to hear them. The office and tidying up the place could wait until the morning; I was too tired.

That night I slept uneasily, with my trusty baseball bat propped up on the mattress.

CHAPTER EIGHT

I was relieved the next morning when I got to the office at nine o'clock sharp, and there was no obvious sign that anybody had been inside. I gave Karl a call and would have been happy to tell him what I had been doing on his behalf over the phone, but he insisted on coming in. We made an appointment for later that morning. I hoped that he wasn't expecting a written report with itemised expenses because this was not my style. I worked out roughly how many hours I had spent so far. While I was waiting for him to arrive, I let myself daydream a bit, about what it would be like to be a real private detective and have a typewriter that worked properly. I had just got to the bit where I had a beautiful secretary that I treated badly, but who loved me just the same, and had traded Merseyside for Miami, when he walked in.

He was wearing a black T-shirt that was three sizes too small, so it emphasised his pecs and biceps. He needn't have bothered because it combined poorly with his jeans and drew your attention to his astronomical beer-belly. I'm such a bitch at heart, but I had decided that I didn't like the man so was justified in passing comment.

I didn't offer my hand, and neither did he as he sat down on the chair opposite.

"What's new, Shannon, have you got anything nice to tell me?"

I noticed that he had dropped the Mr when addressing me and his voice had that slight undertone that gave me the impression that he finished off that sentence in his head with 'Or else I'm gonna kick your teeth in.'

I gave him my best smirk and looked him straight in the eyes. If anything did start between us, I knew which one of us was going down, and it wasn't going be me. Safe in the knowledge that I could take him if I had to, I said as diplomatically as I could, "I think your Billy is in deep shit and that alibi you gave me is a load of old rubbish."

He looked like he was thinking about coming over the desk and throttling me, but the flicker I caught in his eyes only lasted for a second. I continued before he changed his mind. "On the other hand, I've got a few leads that look interesting, and one of them I'm going to see later on today in Dewsbury."

"Fucking Dewsbury? That's a long way. Is it someone that could have killed O'Brian?"

"Anything is possible, Mr Ashford, but that's what I'm getting paid for unless you are unhappy with what I'm doing."

He didn't answer but fixed me again with those cold grey eyes that had the friendliness of an open grave. "How come the warehouse job doesn't give Billy an alibi?"

"The times are all wrong. The police say that whoever it was that did the robbery left at around midnight. The fire didn't happen until much later. I did the maths and drove the distance between Bootle and his house," I lied. "Billy could have finished the job with you, and still had time to kill O'Brian and get back home."

"But he would have told me if he had got any plans to get rid of O'Brian."

I held my hands in the air. "The police are pretty convinced that he had motive and opportunity, so I'm afraid he is still top of their list unless we can prove otherwise."

Before he could interrupt me, I continued talking about the work I had been doing and what Eddie Seer had said about Teresa Savage. At the end, I presented him with a handwritten sheet with my hours written down. If he was impressed, he didn't show it.

He sat for a few seconds as if he was taking in what I had said, and was deciding what to do. In the end, it must have seemed like good sense to continue with me at least for the time being because he hadn't got much else as an alternative. He stood up, peeled off a wad of notes and dropped them on my desk. "Is that enough?"

I counted the amount out in front of him and nodded.

"Ring me when you get something, Shannon." He turned and left without closing the door.

CHAPTER NINE

As I drove the Riley Elf across the Runcorn Bridge and headed on the A5407 towards the Warrington Ring Road, I felt like Detective Crocket from Miami Vice. It was constantly watching that programme that gave me the idea of becoming the Scouse Don Johnson and to set off on a career as a crime fighter. That afternoon as I passed through Oldham and stopped for fish and chips on the outskirts of Huddersfield, I felt that I had finally arrived. A paid job out of town combined with food expenses felt good, and so did the prospect of meeting Julie Carroll. I hoped that she was going to be at home because the money I was on didn't stretch even to the humblest bed and breakfast if I had to stay the night and see her the next day.

I reached Dewsbury late afternoon and pulled into a petrol station to ask directions for the Ravensthorpe District. Warning bells should have started to ring in my head by the look that the petrol pump attendant gave me, but I thought it was because I was a stranger from out of town, and they obviously didn't get many of those here.

Driving around the town, I could see that there wasn't much on offer in terms of eye-catching architectural imagery, but I hadn't come here to go sightseeing. I was picking up a retro-fifties vibe in the way people dressed and drove their vehicles. I skirted the city centre and picked up the A638. When I arrived in Ravensthorpe, it didn't take long for me to find the street where Julie Carroll lived. It was on a pretty drab council estate lined with rows of semi-detached houses that each had small front gardens and privet hedges with more holes than greenery.

It was getting dark and had just started to rain when I walked up the path and rang the bell of number 42 School Terrace. I could see that there was somebody in because there were lights on. I prayed that the local delinquents wouldn't Jack the Elf up and steal its wheels while I was in the house. This was assuming, of course, that this lady was going to let me through the front door.

The bell didn't work, so I tapped on the frosted glass with my car keys. A face appeared through the curtains, and a couple of seconds later, the door opened a fraction; it was on a chain.

I gave her a reassuring smile. This must have been enough to convince her that I was not going to rob or mug her because she closed the door and then opened it again fully. She was in her forties and had wispy mousy brown hair that was cut short, with a couple of strands that hung down in front of her huge brown eyes. She wore a long blue denim skirt with a plain white T-shirt and the sort of tweed cotton slippers that you associate with old people in sheltered accommodation. I needed to show some form of ID, so I thrust my driving licence into her hand and waited while she examined it a little too carefully. Her eyes lingered a bit too long over the part that showed I had got six points for speeding, and I made a mental note to sort out some proper form of identification for the future.

"What are you selling, Mr...?" She looked at the front of my licence. "Shannon?"

"I'm a private detective, and I've been hired to investigate the death of a Mr Tony O'Brian. I believe that you used to know him some time ago."

She handed my licence back, and from her change of expression, I was expecting the door to be closed in my face. Instead, she moved to one side, and I made my way in. I walked down the short hall, and when I entered the lounge, I realised why she wasn't too concerned about letting a stranger into her house. A huge black Doberman ran towards me and started to sniff my crotch area. I froze and backed out into the hall. I hate dogs, but especially big ones that could tear your throat open.

"It's alright, love, let him smell your hand, and he'll be satisfied and go back on his blanket."

I wasn't entirely convinced but held out my hand tentatively, and the dog gave it a lick and went back to the other side of the room. He sat down and watched me before eventually getting bored and lying down. I made a move towards an armchair, and he emitted a low growl, so I stayed where I was and waited for instructions.

"So, it's about Tony? That's a blast from the past." She sat down on the settee and motioned for me to sit down on one of the armchairs.

I kept my eyes on the dog. He was chewing on an old shoe and wasn't interested anymore. I wondered if the shoe was all that was left of her last visitor. "Yes, I'm sorry to have dropped in unannounced, Mrs Carroll."

"That's Miss," she said, lighting up a cigarette. "And call me Julie, everybody else does. How can I help you?"

"Well, I believe that you used to know Mr O'Brian when you were younger. When was the last time that you had any contact with him?"

She ignored my question and went instead for an obvious one she hadn't asked so far. "How did he die?"

I filled her in on the details and repeated my original question.

"I haven't seen Tony since I was living in Belfast, which was when I was eighteen. He was quite a bit older than me." She hesitated, probably wondering if I already knew the story. "I got pregnant, and dad was convinced it was his, and there was a big fight. Tony beat dad up pretty severely. I never saw him after that, but I heard on the grapevine that he had come to live in England."

"You say your dad was convinced it was Tony's baby, but you don't seem so sure. Are you saying it wasn't?"

"I'm saying that my dad was convinced, but you know how it is when you are young. It's all about fun, and you don't give a damn about consequences. I was going out with his mate at first, then started going out with Tony just as I started to miss my periods. Your guess is as good as mine, Mr...?"

"Call me Morris. So, what you're saying is that you were not sure who the father was."

"In a word, yes. Like I said, dad was convinced and ended up in hospital for his trouble."

"Did you have the baby?"

"I had a little boy, but that's about all I can tell you. He was put up for adoption, and I never saw him again. Do you want to stay for dinner, Morris?"

CHAPTER TEN

I sat on a chair in the kitchen and watched Julie make a ham salad. She was still a good-looking woman, and I imagined she must have been a stunner back then in Northern Ireland. She was not unlike an older version of Brigitte Bardot, although her accent was not French but Irish. My arrival at her door and my questions must have stirred up old memories, and they seemed to have put her in a subdued state. She hadn't said very much as she prepared the kitchen table with napkins, placemats and knives and forks.

She worked with a slow precision that was almost hypnotic. She cut and washed iceberg lettuce, shredded carrots, mushrooms and chives, and took the shells off a couple of boiled eggs. She tossed the salad in a big wooden bowl added some oil and tossed it some more. Finally, she placed thick ham on two plates and took some mayonnaise from the fridge, which was in a jam-jar. "I make this myself," she said, smiling. "You must try some on your ham."

She settled into a seat beside me poured steaming black Yorkshire tea into my cup and offered me some thick farmhouse bread and butter. "What sort of work do you do?" I asked through a mouthful of ham.

"I'm a dinner lady at a primary school in town. The money is not that good, but it pays the bills."

"What was Tony like in the old days?"

Julie thought about the question for a while before answering, as if she was trying to remember; "That was a long time ago. He was like any average lad. He drank too much, had sex as often as he could and got into bother with the police once or twice."

She got up, left the room and came back a few minutes later with a photo, which she handed to me. I had been right; she was a stunner when she was younger. The picture was old, dog-eared and in black and white. There were three people in it. Julie was in the middle, and on either side were two boys, probably in their late teens. One of them was a young version of Tony O'Brian, and the other I didn't know.

"I recognise Tony," I said, handing her back the photo, "But who is the other lad?"

"That's Paul McCusker, who I was going with before Tony. He was the love of my life, but he was not as sweet-talking as Tony, plus he was typically quick-tempered. It's true what they say. It's in their blood. When that picture was taken, we were all just mates. It was later when it all got a bit complicated. Don't get me wrong, Tony had a temper, but Paul got mixed up with some bad people, and the writing was on the wall for him. May God rest his poor soul."

I did know what she meant about in the blood. I had a couple of Irish mates, and they all were quick-tempered; "So do you ever see him these days or have you lost touch as well?"

"No, I never saw Paul after I became pregnant, but I heard that he was car bombed in the early days of the troubles. Funny; I always thought he wouldn't make it to thirty, and I was right."

" I take it your dad never liked either of them."

"Dad was a Protestant, and they were Catholic. Do I need to say anymore?"

"Were Paul and Tony involved with any paramilitary groups?"

"Let's put it this way; it was difficult not to be caught up in the emotion between the Catholics and the Protestants. Even though it didn't start properly until long after dad and I had left, you could see it was going that way. Getting back to Yorkshire was like stepping into the future. In Belfast, the Orange Order is still celebrating the Battle of the Boyne, which happened in 1690. We were living in Leeds for a while before moving here, and then dad died, and I've been on my own ever since. I've locked that time we spent out in Belfast away and haven't thought about it for years."

"What about your mum?"

"Died when I was a kid. It's just me now, but I like it that way; with nobody that I have to cook and clean for."

I gave her a hand to clear up the dirty dishes, complimented her on the mayonnaise, and left with a feeling that I may have wasted the trip. I got back to Croxley around ten and called in on Shoddy to see if he was still awake and sober. He surprised me on both counts.

He had updated his easel and had found an address for Teresa Savage, along with all of the other people on the list that worked for O'Brian that Karl Ashford had given me. I told him all about my meeting with Julie Carroll while he made some cocoa.

"So, no joy there, Moggsy, but at least we have got a bit of background information on O'Brian. The thing that I don't understand is where he got the money from to buy the clubs, betting shops and houses. It couldn't all have been from money lending and protection. Something must have happened between the time he was going out with Julie Carroll and when he got here. What was he doing to make all of that money, and how can we find out?"

"Even if we do find out, it still doesn't tell us who killed him."

Shoddy went over to his easel and produced a ruler from off the sideboard. "Okay, so let's assume that Billy didn't kill him. You need a motive for murder, and to make that much money, he must have made some enemies before he came here. The problem we have with that scenario is that if it was someone from out of town, then it is going to be difficult to pick up the pieces and sort them out."

"Are you saying we've got no chance?"

"Well, not much of a chance. If you went to Chester for example and murdered a complete stranger, then left town, you will have probably committed the perfect crime because there are no connections. It's the little connections that throw out a scent that crime investigators can follow. Unless we can pick up the trail, it's going to be difficult, especially with the smell coming off Billy Ashford. It is so obvious that he did it that it is almost too good to be true."

"What about the grown-up son of Julie Carroll, could he have something to do with it?"

Shoddy shook his head. "That's a bit too Agatha Christie for me. What you're saying is that the kid, who was given away, has tracked down his long lost father and killed him. And the motive is what?"

"How do I know? Maybe he is angry at being abandoned, or O'Brian told him that his real father had been blown up, so he wreaks some kind of revenge."

Shoddy pointed at the list on the board. "If we don't turn anything interesting up about Teresa Savage, then maybe this programme on television about drugs has got something to do with his death. It could have been a drugs-related killing, so you should check out the people on the list that Karl Ashford gave you and see if there is a drugs angle. If that fails, then we come to yet another brick wall."

I let myself out, after saying goodnight to Shoddy. I wasn't feeling as optimistic at the end of the day as I had felt at the start. I took a beer out of the fridge and sat out on my balcony drinking it from the bottle. It didn't go down well after cocoa, and I crawled into bed around one o'clock with a pain in my stomach and my head spinning with facts about the case. As detectives go, I realised I wasn't up there with the likes of Holmes or Poirot, but then again they were fictional and didn't have a client like Karl Ashford, and a drunk as a sidekick. I hoped that Karl didn't feel inclined to ask for his money back. I wished that like in all the best detective stories, some sort of clue would turn-up because sure as hell I needed a break.

CHAPTER ELEVEN

There was a message from Eddie Seer on the answerphone at the office the next morning. He told me that it wasn't urgent, but I called him back anyway. It seemed that all he wanted was a beer and a chat about old times, so I arranged to meet him later in The Hundred for a liquid lunch.

I did a bit of tidying up and called Clair Ashford to see if she had any news about Billy. I got through to her answer phone and left a message to call me back when she had a minute. I arrived at the pub at midday. Eddie was already there and had bought me a pint. We shook hands, and thankfully he didn't pat me this time, although he did give me a few playful digs in my stomach, which I hated. He was dressed in faded Levis, denim shirt and Wrangler jacket that had all seen better days. He looked a lot younger out of his tuxedo but just as hard.

"Still doing the martial arts?" I asked as we took our drinks into the snug, which as usual was empty.

"Still sitting in your favourite chair?" He retaliated with a smirk.

I sat down in another one just to spite him, but it didn't feel right so got up and sat down in my usual spot. "Are you married, or are you still shagging young girls around the clubs?"

"I'm not married, but I'm getting a bit long in the tooth for young girls, Moggsy. These days I concentrate on my Krav Maga techniques." He did some vague martial art movements with his hands and threw a punch with lightning speed that stopped a whisker away from my nose.

I felt pleased with myself that I hadn't flinched and took a mouthful of beer. "That looks nasty, Ed, what is it, some kind of oriental shenanigans for tossers who can't get a hard-on?"

He laughed. "No, it's a combination of judo, wrestling, boxing, jujutsu and street fighting. It was developed by the Israelis, and you know how mad those lads are. I picked it up while I was in the Middle East on detachment to one of their units, and it's sort of grown on me ever since. Funnily enough, I have just taken a grading, and I'm now a fifth Dan. What about you, Moggsy, are you still keeping yourself fit?"

"Not really; too many chips and late nights. I still rely on the old Shannon Leer to scare the bastards off that want to mess." I made a scary face, and he smiled politely

He asked me if I had got round to seeing Teresa Savage yet, and I filled him in on the details of what Julie Carroll had told me. Apparently, Eddie had served in Northern Ireland for a time, so I name-dropped, Paul McCusker. He shook his head and said that the name didn't ring a bell. It seemed that when I came to anything even vaguely connected to O'Brian's death, nobody knew anything, so I gave him my list of names to see if there was anything that he might know to help me.

Eddie studied the names. "To be honest, Moggsy, I can't see what any of this lot has got to do with what happened to O'Brian. Alice Stewart is nineteen and works in the cloakroom, Colin Dicks, and Andy Thomas manage the betting shops and are likely to lose their jobs now Carney is in charge so don't have anything to gain." He looked carefully at the last name and stroked his chin. "Pete Farrell is the ex-owner of the Kabin, so you never know, he might have a grudge."

"What happened to the owner of the Oasis?"

"I think he moved to Spain or Portugal, but I know Farrell still lives local, so he could be worth a try."

"Where you working the door when they made the TV programme about drugs being sold in the Oasis and the Kabin?"

"No, I started a bit after, but I can tell you that the whole show didn't go down well with a lot of people around here and O'Brian was furious. There were a couple of small-time drug dealers in the club when I first started at the Oasis. You know the score, Moggsy. You keep your eye on it, and as long as it doesn't get out of control, you leave them to it and look for the real troublemakers. A few dopeheads don't cause problems; it's the drunks that are looking for a fight at the end of the night.

"Have you got any names?"

"I haven't, mate, but maybe I can ask around for you. The strange thing is that there were always one or two dealers selling drugs when I got the job, but a little while after it just stopped altogether. That's true for both clubs. O'Brian purged the bastards, and I can hold my hand on my heart and say that his clubs had become drug-free zones."

We drank until closing time and couldn't persuade any of the bar staff to let us stay, so I drove off to see if I could find Teresa Savage and Eddie headed home.

The address I'd been given was just out of town in a posh Greenbelt zone before you reached the motorway, called Springdale Lodge. People in Croxley call the area Legoland because all of the houses are the same, and all of the people who live in them are professional types. These are the people who couldn't afford a house in an expensive area like the Wirral. Springdale is an oddity, which with a bit of imagination could have been picturesque. Just being in Legoland was like driving with an acute déjà-vu condition because as you went around every corner, you got the distinct impression you had been there before. Nothing separated the monotony except the street names, which were pretty lame. I had just come down JFK Drive and turned into Martin Luther Avenue for the second time. I was beginning to doubt that Bill Haley Close existed. I finally saw the half-obscured name as I went past, for the third time and had to reverse back to drive down it.

It was half-past four and going dark when I pulled up outside the front gate of number eleven, and the Close looked deserted. The residents were probably still at work, and would all arrive together around 6 o'clock. Number eleven was a Mock Tudor semi-detached building with red herringbone brickwork. There was an insipid black and white timber-effect on the upper floor, and the windows had so many small panes of glass that they must have been a bitch to clean. I imagined that inside there would be fake wooden beams to give the impression you were living in a property that had history, but without the downside of bad plumbing, rising damp, and rats.

I opened the gate of the small, well-kept garden, walked up the drive with a miniature hedge on either side and knocked on the door. I wasn't optimistic about anybody being in because there were no lights on and no car in the drive, but I gave it five minutes before peering in through the lounge window. The curtains were open, and the room from what I could see was expensively furnished. I tried to get around to the back, but there was a high wooden gate that was locked. I gave up and walked back to my car. I settled myself in and waited.

It wasn't long before a car pulled up to the drive of the house next door to number eleven, and a middle-aged lady got out and began to open the double gates. I got out and caught up with her before she got back into her car. As I got closer, I could see that there were a couple of teenagers sitting in the back. She stood behind the open car door using it as a barrier between us and waited for me to say something.

"I don't suppose you know what time the lady at number eleven gets in?"

"Terry?"

I nodded my head.

"Are you a friend of hers?"

"No, I'm from the Oasis club where she used to work. I need to talk to her about..." I should have thought this one through, but it's all part of the detecting learning process. "About her back pay."

Another car pulled up to the curb, and this time a man got out and started opening the gate to the drive of number nine. The lady I was talking to shook her head. "She is usually home quite late. Dave," she shouted across. "What time does Terry finish her shift at the Fourways?"

The man, who was in the process of getting back in his car, shouted. "Haven't got a clue, but late" and drove up his drive.

The lady shook her head and got back into her car. "Sorry I can't be more helpful."

I walked back to my car and got in. The lady had been helpful enough. The only Fourways that I knew in the area was the Fourways Hotel, near the airport. Of course, it could have been the

Fourways Dry Cleaners or the Fourways Chinese Takeaway, but I doubt if they had any shift-workers. I was due for a break, so I started the engine and headed for Speke.

CHAPTER TWELVE

The Fourways isn't exactly an airport hotel, but it is close enough to pick up passenger traffic, and a lot of flight crews on stopovers. It had a reputation with the local lads as a great spot for pulling air hostesses. The hotel itself is a nondescript grey rectangle four-story eyesore that has got around 40 rooms and is rated as a three-star.

From outside, it looked devoid of life and empty, but as I entered through the revolving doors into the surprisingly bright and spacious reception area that couldn't have been further from the truth. The lobby was buzzing with people all with pull-along overnight cases. I suspected that I was in for a long wait before I could get to talk to one of the three staff behind the desk and find out if Teresa Savage worked here. She could be one of them. I discounted the man and examined the other two: a blonde and a redhead. The blonde girl could not have been more than 22 and was too pretty to be the person Eddie had described, but the redhead fitted into the imaginary picture I had already formed in my head of what Teresa Savage should look like.

She was around five foot two, with short red hair that was cut into a pageboy style, and skin so white it didn't look as if it had ever spent any time out of doors. From the bits of her I could see above the desk, she was wearing a white blouse with a nametag pinned on that was too small for me to read. Her bright red lipstick and heavily made-up eyes made her look older than she most likely was. I guessed that would be around thirty. She looked calm under pressure, but there was something about a combination of red hair and green eyes that said when this lady got angry, you had better get out of the way in a hurry. She looked a bit too bossy to be my type of woman, but I certainly wouldn't have kicked her out of bed if there were no other options, and I had drunk a few whiskies.

The three of them were working fast, and the guests were being dispatched through the checking-in process quickly and efficiently. As I was getting closer, I got a good look at her nametag. It said, Teresa. Maybe my luck had changed at last.

I had to let a lady who was behind me, take my turn, as the blonde became free and smiled for me to come forward. I smiled back and shook my head. I moved directly in front of Teresa, who was trying to make a man who was either German or Dutch, understand that he didn't need to pay there and then, but when he checked out. She had a Northern Irish accent, and although she was smiling, her eyes were sending out dark signals.

Finally, the old man was heading towards the lift, and she turned those sparkling green eyes on me. There was only one other person checking in now, and the blonde had wandered off into the back office. The man was busy giving directions to a stunning air hostess and flirting so badly and noticeably it was embarrassing.

Teresa smiled and said in a sing-song voice "How can I help you tonight, sir?"

"Are you, Teresa Savage?" I asked

That took the smile off her face, but she recovered quickly. "I'm sorry, but I don't think we have met."

"I'm a private investigator that is looking into the death of Tony O'Brian, would it be possible for me to have a few minutes of your time?"

She looked at the other receptionist who was still trying to pull the air hostess and wasn't taking any notice of us. "Look, I'm sorry, but I'm at work as you can see, and anyway, I don't think that there is much I can say. I didn't know him that well."

"I'm talking to people who even knew him slightly. It will only take a few minutes of your time and could help me a lot."

She lowered her voice "Look, you little prick. I've got nothing to say, and anyway, you're not even police, so there's no law that says I have to." She thought for a second and added under her breath. "And who the fuck hired you anyway?"

I had to knock her out of her comfort zone, so I raised my voice. "Murder is a very serious business, Teresa."

She grabbed my arm and ushered me to the far side of the desk. "Okay, I can give you ten minutes but not here." On cue, another wave of people came through the swing doors.

"I'm not working tomorrow, so why not come over to my house and I'll tell you what little I know." She picked up a pad, wrote her address down and handed it to me. "Come around about nine tomorrow night." She moved away, switched on her meet-and-greet smiley face, and totally blanked me out. I wasn't too bothered by that because I had got what I wanted. I walked back to my car and headed for home.

I popped into the office on my way back to the flat and saw the red light on my answerphone flashing, which meant I had a message. I was hoping it was going to be from Clair Ashford, but in fact, it was from Eddie. He had got some information on one of the kids that used to deal drugs in the Oasis. Someone called Deggsy, who drank at a pub called the Dockers Arms, which wasn't too far away by car. I looked at the time. It was just after ten o'clock. If I was quick, I could round off the night with a chat to this lowlife and have a few well-earned beers.

CHAPTER THIRTEEN

By the time I got to the Dockers, it was a quarter to eleven. I pulled into a side street, parked -up and went into the bar, which was full of kids in various stages of intoxication. The pub was the centre of Croxley's vibrant drugs and music scene, and I could hear a local rock band playing badly in the function room on the first floor directly above us. The noise made the windows and light fittings shake and stopped any meaningful conversation.

I ordered a beer at the top of my voice and mingled. This was definitely one of the pubs I would not have usually been seen dead in, and I was getting some odd looks from a couple of the lads in there. I was wearing my usual dark grey suit, tweed tie, and anorak, so maybe they thought I was the police, or even worse, an insurance salesman. Either way, the vibe I was picking up made me want to finish my drink and leave before something started with my name on it.

I had a look in the games room, which was at the far end of the bar. It was small and packed with young lads standing around the two pool tables. The air was thick with smoke, and there was a serious smell of marijuana. I asked a boy standing by the door, with a pool cue in his hand if Deggsy was in tonight, and he just looked at me as if I was a retard, shook his head, and went over to the table to play his shot. I stayed near the door toying with my drink and was relieved when the music stopped as it was giving me a headache. Simultaneously there was a shout from the other room that it was last orders. I rushed automatically like everybody else to the bar to get a final drink. As I was paying, I asked the landlord if Deggsy was in, and without hesitation, he pointed to a suedehead revivalist coming out of the games room with an empty glass in his hand.

He could hardly be described as a kid, and I clocked him as being about twenty-three. He was on his own, but I remembered he had been one of the lads playing pool and had stuck in my memory because he was almost as tall as me, but thin as a stick and covered in tattoos.

I cut him off before he could get to the bar. "Are you, Deggsy?"

"Are you Police?" He countered and sidestepped around me.

I watched him hold his glass out to one of the barmaids, and went back to the bar and stood by him. "Can I buy that one for you?"

"Are you trying to pick me up, pal?" He said, handing his money over and taking his drink, without looking at me.

"I'm a private detective, looking into the murder of Tony O'Brian. Do you think you could give me five minutes to answer a couple of questions?"

"I can't help you, mate. I don't know the man, now fuck off will yer, if you don't want to get your head kicked in."

I grabbed his arm, and he shrugged it off and pushed passed me toward the games room without a backwards glance.

It was an easy choice of following after him and getting nasty with the little runt or finishing my drink and going home. It was no contest. I finished my drink and made for the door. Outside, there was a white transit van pulled up on the pavement, with members of the band I'd heard playing, loading up.

I had only gone a little way past them when I picked up the sound of running feet behind me, and as I turned around to see what was happening, suede head ran past and pushed me. I lost my balance and fell against the pub wall, and they were on me like a pack of wolves in a second, kicking, and punching. I instinctively rolled over into the foetal position and tried to cover my head. There were about five of them, and the last one to run off into the night was Deggsy, the half skinhead. Before he disappeared, he spat on me aimed a kick between my legs and shouted, "You're dead if I see you here again, wanker."

I rolled over, put my back against the wall and breathed in and out deeply. One of the members of the band came over and asked me if I was okay, and I assured him that I wasn't in too much pain. In fact, I wasn't badly hurt, and the kicking I had taken looked a lot worse than it was. I had taken the brunt of the blows on my arms, and they were wearing regular shoes, not bovver boots, so there was nothing broken. I still checked before getting up.

I wasn't injured but was as angry as hell. I half walked, half ran to the Elf, and set off in the direction Deggsy and his mates had gone. It took no more than five minutes to catch up with them. I turned my lights off and pulled into the curb behind an industrial skip that had been left on the street, and was full of rubble. I got out of the car and hid in the shadows watching.

There were four of them sitting on a ledge and leaning against the window of a Chinese takeaway with food trays in their hands. They were eating, smoking and laughing. Giving me a kicking had given them an adrenalin rush, which had more than likely been the high point of their weekend. I already knew that I was going to spoil the weekend for one of them, but I hoped that I was going to get the opportunity to do it quickly, as I was ready for my bed.

I locked the car and waited, and after about fifteen minutes of chat, they threw their cans and food trays on the floor, kicked them about for a bit, and then walked off down the road. I followed on foot from a safe distance. Part of the detective course that I did was about tailing suspects and how to avoid being seen. It's not as easy as it looks, and in an ideal situation should be done by three or four people who continually change places with each other. I remember that one of the rules stated it was crucial to use a crowd as cover while rule number four was to synchronise your steps with your mark so that he can't hear your footsteps. Nothing like that was going to work tonight, and I was relying on the fact that my mark was so stuck up his own arse, and so full of alcohol and drugs that I could have been holding his hand, and he wouldn't have noticed me.

I think rule three was not to get distracted, or complacent, and always expect the unexpected. They suddenly began running, jumping on cars and walking over the roofs and bonnets setting off the alarms. I obviously couldn't try to blend in by doing the same, so I had to run as fast as I could while staying a safe distance and keeping low so as not to be seen. I must have got too low because as I emerged from behind a parked up lorry, three of the lads had disappeared, and it was just Deggsy walking on his own. So there was a god after all.

I followed him for another ten minutes before he turned into a side street that led to a block of two-storey flats. He walked up the stairs, and I lost sight of him for a couple of seconds before he appeared again on the second level. I watched as he walked along the communal balcony and let himself into one of the flats. I counted back, and it was seventh in the row, with a brown door. A light went on, and I waited and watched for a while, and after twenty minutes, the light went out, so I walked back to my car.

I drove the Elf to the flats and parked in a spot roughly adjacent to Deggsy's flat, and got out. I walked up the stairs and counted the doors until I came to number seven. I took a deep breath, then kicked it in, walked into the hall and closed it behind me as best I could. There was a light underneath the door at the far end of the corridor, and I rushed towards it and entered the room. Deggsy was standing up looking drowsy, in a vest and boxer shorts. He must have been asleep on the sofa, but the noise had startled him awake. When he saw me come through the door, I could see that nothing had registered yet on his face, so I pushed my advantage and hit him in the gut. He went down with a gasp. I sat on his chest, grabbed his right hand, and pressed my leg over his other one so that he couldn't take a swing at me.

"Hi, Deggsy, do you remember me?"

He was waking up a bit now and began to struggle, but he wasn't strong, and I had no problem holding him. I could see the fear in his eyes, which I knew was going to make my job easier. I grabbed hold of his index finger and began to twist it back, and he started screaming with pain.

"It's going to break in a minute, Deggsy, are you sure you don't want to have that little chat now?"

He screamed some more as I increased the pressure and shouted "Okay."

I eased off, but still held onto the finger. "Did you sell drugs at the Oasis and Kabin for Karl and Billy Ashford?"

He nodded his head.

"Why did you stop?"

"I don't know; I just did."

"Wrong answer, you lying little twat." I began to twist his finger back.

He shouted, "Okay, I was barred from getting in."

"So what did Karl and Billy have to say about that?"

"Billy said he was going to sort it out."

I maintained just enough pressure on the finger for him to understand that if I applied anymore, it was going to snap. "How do you mean sort it out?"

"How the hell do I know?"

I applied more pressure on the finger, and he screamed in agony "I don't fucking know; honest."

I let his finger go and got up. Deggsy sat up holding it. There were tears in his eyes; either because of the pain or the hatred he was probably feeling at that moment towards me. I wasn't sure which and to be honest didn't care.

"Thanks for taking to time, to talk to me, kiddo," I said, walking to the door. "Don't worry; I'll let myself out."

I couldn't have been in Deggsy's flat more than five minutes, and as I drove home I realised how lucky I had been that he either lived alone or the people he shared with were too scared to come out of the bedroom and see what was going on. I don't like violence, but sometimes it has got its uses, and tonight was one of them. I felt that I had got my first breakthrough, although rather than put Billy in the clear; it put him further in the shit. My brain was too tired to work out the full implications of what I had learnt tonight, but at least it was something for Shoddy to write on his easel.

It was past one o'clock when I got home, and I was surprised to see a note pinned to my door from the man himself, telling me to give him a knock when I got back. It had been a long day, and I was tired but intrigued to see what news he had that would be so urgent. Shoddy opened the door on my third knock, just as I was about to give up and get to bed. He looked as if he had just woken up, but he held the door open and ushered me in.

"What's happened?"

He went over to the table, picked up a piece of paper and handed it to me. "Take a look at this; it's an incident report on the day of the murder. A police car was called to the Oasis club at three o'clock in the afternoon to investigate a disturbance."

The paper was a photocopy, and split into three sections; the Detail section outlined that a police car had been summoned to the Oasis Club car park at three o'clock on October the 21st, where an argument was taking place between Billy Ashford and Tony O'Brian. Ashford was acting in a violent manner and had to be restrained by the officers. He was allowed to leave the scene after calming down, and O'Brian was asked if he wanted to press charges but declined. The only other witness to the incident, and the person who had dialled 999 was Teresa Savage. She had made a short statement to the officers at the scene, stating that Billy had threatened to kill O'Brian, and had used aggressive behaviour, though no actual physical violence had occurred. Under the section entitled Action Taken, was written no further action, and in the summary, there was just some technical police jargon that I skipped.

Things were looking up. "How the hell did you get this, mate?"

"Don't ask, Moggsy, but it certainly looks bad for Billy."

I told him about my day, and what I had found out, and he made us both tea and toast, before going over to his easel and updating the information we had got so far. It was beginning to take shape, though from the point of view of the Ashfords was not so great.

Shoddy got out his ruler, and I sat down and munched toast and marmalade.

"It looks as though the tip-off that the police had received, to put them onto Billy so quickly was this incident, and the anonymous caller was Teresa Savage. The report doesn't say what the argument was about between the two of them, and either Teresa Savage didn't know, or she wasn't telling. There are two possibilities. The first is about the relationship between O'Brian and Clair Ashford, which as far as we know finished, if it ever actually started, a couple of years ago. If Billy was going to do something about it, I think he would have done it before, though it still could be a possible motive, especially if Clair Ashford is lying. What is more likely is that it was something to do with what you found out tonight about O'Brian not allowing the Ashfords to sell drugs in the Kabin and the Oasis."

"But how hard would that hurt the Ashfords financially? It surely was not enough for Billy to kill him."

"We all know Billy's reputation for having a quick temper and being a nasty piece of work, Moggsy, but who can say for sure. Maybe, it was a combination of both the drugs and the rumoured affair with his wife. That's why it's important to speak to Teresa Savage. If she knows what they argued about, then it's a big help in getting to the bottom of whether it was enough to kill for. If the Ashfords let O'Brian get away with this, then it looks like a sign of weakness, so it might have something to do with saving face."

"Teresa Savage didn't tell the police about why the argument took place, so why should she tell me?"

"You're going to have to use your charm, Moggs; who knows? She might pour her heart out to you. In the meantime, I'll see if I can dig anything up on her that we can use as leverage. Where did you say that she was working now?"

I filled him in on the details and said goodnight. I was bushed, but as usual, couldn't get to bed without having a beer on my balcony to wind down. The more I found out, the guiltier Billy seemed. It wasn't the result that Karl wanted, and I hoped that he was going to understand that I was only doing my job, but I very much doubted it.

CHAPTER FOURTEEN

I was up early the next morning and in the office for ten o'clock. There were a lot of loose ends that I wanted to tie up before I went to see Teresa Savage; things such as itemising my bill by working out the hours that I had spent on the case so far. I wanted to seem more professional than I actually was, and realised that I needed to invest in a typewriter.

I was in the middle of making a cup of tea when the door burst open and in walked Karl Ashford. He didn't look in a very good mood and didn't bother closing it behind him. I hate aggressive behaviour, especially first thing in the morning before I'd completely woken up. I tried to diffuse the anger waves that were coming off him with a pleasant smile. It didn't seem to work.

"What the fuck have you been up to, Shannon?" He shouted at me.

I shook my head "In what sense, Mr Ashford?"

"In the sense that you seem to be going around trying to blame Billy, rather than find the person who killed O'Brian."

The penny dropped, "I'm assuming here that you are talking about my meeting with Deggsy last night. Do you want to get to the truth, or are you just sticking your head in the sand? Just because he's your brother doesn't mean that he didn't have anything to do with killing O'Brian, and the argument that they had earlier on in the day didn't help either. This is an argument, by the way, that you chose not to tell me about."

That did it, and I could almost hear something inside him snap. He ran at me, grabbed my lapels and tried a head-butt. Maybe in his heyday, Karl could have inflicted some damage on my nose with his head, but now even though he still looked the part, he was too old, too slow, and too obvious with his technique. I pushed my hands between his and brought them back, forcing him to release his grip, and probably hurting his fingers in the process. I stepped back and hit him with a left hook.

I finished making my tea as I was waiting for him to come around and put another tea bag in a spare mug in case he wanted one. The bastard had bruised my knuckles with his face, and I was going to have to put some antiseptic cream on them later.

He regained consciousness slowly and got up rubbing his chin. I handed him the tea, which he took, and I gestured for him to sit down. I offered him sugar, but he shook his head, and I sat down at my desk opposite him.

"Right, Mr Ashford, shall we be civilised and pretend that what just happened didn't take place, and you have just walked calmly into my office and sat down. Now; what is the purpose of your visit this morning?"

He shifted in his chair uncomfortably and rubbed his chin again. "Billy didn't kill O'Brian. If he had, I would have been the first to know." He crossed two of his fingers, "We were that close. There is just no way."

"So, what about this argument with O'Brian in the afternoon of the murder. Did you know anything about it?"

"I knew he had been to see O'Brian, but it was no big deal. Billy just said that he was being an arsehole and laughed it off. We were both going to go and see him again the next day."

"Is this anything to do with him banning drugs in his clubs?"

"We always got on good with O'Brian. He let us sell a bit of puff in his clubs, and we kept out any other dealers. We also did a bit of work for him in the early days."

"You mean when he was working the protection racket?"

Karl's body language looked like he wanted to hit me again, but he relaxed and took a sip of his tea. "Yeah, if you like. What I'm saying is that until he started being a twat, everything was okay. For no reason, he became heavy and started banning my lads from his clubs. We just wanted to know why."

"I had a peek at the police incident report, and Billy was pretty aggressive in the car park of the Oasis. He said he was going to kill O'Brian according to a witness."

"Billy said a lot of things, Shannon; he had that sort of personality, but what we made off selling drugs in those clubs was beer money. We did the job in Bootle, and he didn't even mention the guy, except to say that I should come with him the next day. He wouldn't have said that if he was planning on killing him. It just doesn't make sense."

As I drove through the Birkenhead tunnel on my way to see Peter Farrell, who now lived in New Brighton, I had to admit that it did seem strange for Billy to want to kill O'Brian for such a silly reason. Something was not right about it, especially if Billy had planned to go with Karl to sort it out the next day. There had to be something else that I was missing. I hoped that my meeting with Teresa Savage would answer some of my questions.

Pete Farrell, the ex-owner of the Kabin Nightclub, was the only person that I had phoned that morning who had been in, and he agreed to meet me at his home after lunch. His house was up one of the many side streets off the Promenade and was one of those huge Victorian structures with three floors and a basement that had once been graced by the families of wealthy Liverpool Merchants. Unfortunately, those good-time days had long gone, and now, a lot of the houses had been turned into dingy bed and breakfasts, and there were one or two that had been boarded up. Even in the bright winter sunshine, there was an air of neglect about the New Brighton area, and I couldn't imagine why someone would be living here by choice.

A thin lady with white hair done up in a bun, who I assumed was Farrell's wife, opened the door. She was friendly enough and showed me down some steps into a basement room that smelt of damp and pipe tobacco. She told me to take a seat and that Mr Farrell would be with me in a minute, and left. The room was small with an old oak desk against one wall, a couple of chairs and nothing else. The wood-chip wallpaper was smoke-stained with age, and there was a pile of old newspapers going yellow stacked up in the corner, with a load of brown cardboard boxes tied up with string nearby.

What natural light there was came from a large bay window that looked upwards through grey net drapes that weren't hung very well, and green railings on to the pavement outside. I looked out of the window. There was a lorry parked up across the street with three workmen trying to unload a settee.

"You must be, Mr Shannon."

I spun around and took hold of the outstretched hand being offered. It was dry and bony but had the exaggerated firmness of a high-pressure car salesman that wanted to make you think he was honest. Peter Farrell looked like a college professor, with a mass of mad grey hair, and piercing blue eyes behind Mr Magoo spectacles. He was tall and slim and had the sort of high cheek-boned face that didn't give his age away, though I would have guessed by the look of his wife that he must have been at least seventy. He was smoking a Sherlock Holmes pipe, with the bowl carved into the face of an Indian, which he waved in the general direction of a seat by his desk. I sat down, and he sat down behind it and started playing with his pipe, as pipe smokers tend to do in moments of stress.

"So what can I do for you, Mr Shannon? I know you said it was something to do with the unfortunate incident involving Mr O'Brian, but I don't see how I fit in." He had a southern accent, and from his posture, I had the impression that he had spent some time in the military.

Before I could answer, his wife came into the room carrying a silver tray, with a teapot, two cups and milk and sugar on it. She put it on the desk and poured out the tea without asking if I wanted one.

Farrell stopped poking the bowl of his pipe, put it down in the ashtray and took one of the cups. "Milk and sugar, Mr Shannon?" He asked

"No, I like it as it comes."

I waited for his wife to leave before speaking. "I believe that you were the owner of the Kabin nightclub before Tony O'Brian took it over. Would I be right in saying that you weren't very happy selling?"

He made a sound in between a laugh and a cough. "I was getting too old for the club game, and Tony made me a substantial offer, which I took, and that's about it. There were no threats if that's what you mean."

"So when was the last time that you saw him?"

"Oh, let me see. That would be when I sold the club. I moved out here and retired. I never go back to Croxley that much these days, because there's no need."

"I heard that he had a few rackets on the go when he first arrived in town. Are you saying that you never heard anything?"

"I did hear that he had been accused of operating a loan sharking business, but like I said, he always played fair with me, so I've got no complaints."

I wasn't getting anywhere with this guy. If he was lying, he was doing it while looking me straight in the eyes. If he was telling the truth, then this must have been another Tony O'Brian we were talking about. I served him my last question and watched his face carefully. "How did you feel when you heard that he had been murdered?"

There was not a flicker. "I read the news like everybody else. Nobody deserves to die like that, Mr Shannon, and I hope whoever did it gets put away for a very long time."

"They say it was Billy Ashford. Did you ever have any dealings with him or his brother Karl while you owned the Kabin?" Did I detect a slight change of body language at the mention of the

Ashfords, or was it just my hyped-up imagination? Whatever it might have been, he recovered quickly.

"I really can't remember. I dealt with lots of people when I ran the club. I wish I could be of more help." He made a move to get up, and I got the hint.

Walking down the street from his house towards the promenade, I heard footsteps approaching quickly behind me, and I instinctively moved to one side to let whoever it was pass. Mrs Farrell came up beside me half walking, half running with an Irish setter on a lead that was pulling her down the street. "Have you got a minute, Mr Shannon?" She was out of breath and held the lead with two hands. "There's a cafe at the end of the road. We could go in there." With that, she let the dog off the lead, and he ran off towards the beach.

"He's got a lot of energy. Will he come back?"

We watched the dog disappear around the corner. "Yes, he just goes up the promenade, and then comes home when he gets tired." She had stopped beside a small cafe that had steamed up windows, and a board outside advertising all-day breakfast. I opened the door for her. Inside was empty except for a lady sitting at the side of the counter reading the Daily Mirror with a cigarette hanging from her mouth. I ordered two cups of tea from her, and we sat down at a table next to the window.

I got straight to the point as we were waiting for the tea to arrive. "What have you got for me, Mrs Farrell?"

"It's Val, and Peter is not my husband; he is my younger brother." She added; "A lot of people make that mistake."

The tea arrived, and I waited for the waitress to leave before continuing. "Are you or Peter married?"

"Well, in a way, we were both married to the business, and we didn't have time for much else. It was my dad's club before we took it over, but of course, it changed a lot in the 60s because before, it was more of a dancehall than a club. Dad got ill, and Peter had just got out of the army, so it seemed logical that we ran it as a family business. Back then, we had live bands on two floors and a restaurant that served curry, chips and a cup of coffee, which was included in the price of the ticket. We were making good money, and then Tony O'Brian arrived in Croxley."

"But your brother said that he wanted to sell, and the offer O'Brian made was very generous."

"That's not as it was, but Peter doesn't want to get involved after all this time, with raking up the past."

"And you?"

She leaned forward, her face intense "I don't forget so quickly, Mr Shannon. That man and his cronies destroyed our life, and I would have killed him myself if I thought that I could get away with it."

"What happened?"

"It started off all business-like with a meeting between him and us. He made us an offer that we refused. About a week later, those two Ashford brothers..."

"Billy and Karl?"

"Yes. I eavesdropped on your conversation with Peter. Those two turned up at the club and told Peter that if he didn't agree to sell, they were going to kill me."

"What did you do? Did you contact the police?"

"We thought about it, but things escalated rather quickly. When we got home that night, our dog, Rusty, was lying dead on the floor of the hall without his head. We found the head the next morning in the office at the club, and to be perfectly frank with you, Mr Shannon, it frightened us. Just the fact that they could get in our house and the Kabin so easily made us think that calling the police was futile."

"Is that when you decided to sell?"

"I wanted to try and do something, but losing the dog broke Peter's heart, and I could see that he just wanted to get rid of the club. There were other incidents after that, with lots of fights, staff leaving and finally, Peter's car being set on fire in the car park. We contacted O'Brian, who said that the offer had gone down to half of what he originally agreed to pay, but we accepted anyway."

"O'Brian took over a lot of businesses and property when he first arrived in town, do you think he did the same to them as he did to you?"

"I know that the owner of the Oasis, Alex Thompson, was threatened, and his wife was invalided after she was run over on a zebra crossing, around the same time. Alex sold and moved abroad soon after." She took a sip of tea. "I just wanted you to know that Billy Ashford is capable of killing, and O'Brian was definitely worth killing, so in my book justice has finally been done. It doesn't help Alex Thompson or us very much, but at least he can't do what he did to us, to anybody else.

There was not much that I could say after what she had told me. Obviously, both of the Ashfords and O'Brian were low life and deserved all that they got. The fact that I was working for Karl was nothing I was proud of, especially as I didn't need the money. I left some cash on the table for the tea, and we walked out together. The dog came rushing back to greet her, and I watched them both as they made their way home up the street.

When I got back to my flat, I knocked on Shoddy's door, but he was out, so I settled in on the settee with a couple of beers and watched afternoon television. It wasn't long before I was asleep.

CHAPTER FIFTEEN

Shoddy woke me up, knocking on the door at five o'clock. He was standing outside my flat with a smug look on his face. I followed him into his place eager to find out what nugget of knowledge he had dug up. It had to be a good one because he milked my impatience by insisting on making a cup of tea for us both before he started. When he was ready he handed me my tea and a plate of bourbon creams and I settled down to listen as he picked up his ruler and went over to the easel. It was crammed with information.

"I did a fair bit of digging around today, Moggsy; to see if could find anything about Teresa Savage. I got nowhere until I remembered that you said she had a Northern Ireland accent. I've got a mate who works in the RUC in Belfast, and I gave him a ring. He couldn't tell me anything off the top of his head but said he would do some checking. He got back to me about an hour ago. Apparently, Savage is her married name, which she kept even though she is now divorced.

The suspense was killing me. "So what's her maiden name?"

"It's McCusker; she's the sister of Paul McCusker, who was killed in a car bomb incident over there in the 1970s."

"Well, that certainly gives the whole thing a twist. It could also open the door for a lot of reasons why O'Brian was killed."

"You mean an Irish connection?"

"They obviously must have all known each other, and that's why O'Brian probably gave her a job. It could also explain the reason she never went back to work after he was killed, and was so angry when I turned up."

Shoddy shook his head and took a swig of tea. "I'm sorry; Moggs, but I don't like it. Dealing with people like the Ashfords is one thing, but this is the IRA we are talking about. They're a terrorist organisation that is not motivated by money. Idealists are dangerous."

"We don't know that yet, and it was a long time ago."

"As far as we know; but we can't say for certain what O'Brian has been up to, or if he was working for someone. My advice would be just to let the whole thing drop. You've given Karl his money's worth so he can't complain. Just write him a report and say that's as far as you can go."

It was tempting but I suppose I am like a cat at heart and when I get involved in something my curiosity overrides any self-preservation instincts. I tried to change the subject. "What else did you find out?"

Shoddy gave me one of his withering looks. "That's not enough for you? Well, my friend accessed her file for me and, apparently, when she was younger she had been quite busy but never enough to get her arrested. It was thought that she was used as a honey trap to lure Protestants with promises of sex to a place where her brother,

Pau,l would then beat the shit out of them. He is digging out more information on Paul McCusker and O'Brian but it's going to take a while." He added. "I knew that you wouldn't let this case go but I thought that I had better ask just to be sure."

I filled him in on what I had got from Farrell and his sister and he spent a few minutes updating his easel.

"It looks as though O'Brian has made a good few enemies in his lifetime but which one did he hurt enough for them to kill him in such a brutal fashion. To do that to his skull shows that it was somebody that hated him."

I interrupted, "D you don't think it could have been something to do with what he'd been up to in Ireland?"

"Well, until we get some information from my mate out there it is stupid to speculate. If he was involved with the IRA, then it could be a killing by a Protestant Para-Military group like the UDA, but it's a long time to wait for a revenge killing if you ask me."

"So, we are back to square one."

"It depends on what you were expecting, Moggsy. One thing is for certain, and that is if you are mad enough to cut a dog's head off as a warning, you wouldn't have a problem with smashing up a man's skull with a sledgehammer. The fact that Billy and Karl both worked for O'Brian and that there was an argument, still points the finger firmly at Billy I'm afraid, mate."

"What about Teresa turning out to be McCusker's sister?"

"It could be relevant but that depends on what she tells you tonight. I would not give your hand away straight away. Let her talk and see what she knows. The fact that they knew each other in Belfast could be the key to everything but could also be an irrelevant red herring."

"Great! So the only progress that we've made is to confirm how guilty Billy is."

"That's the way it looks, though it could be that the Farrell pair have got something to hide. They have a motive, and who knows what connections he has from his military days." Shoddy wrote the names, Peter and Val Farrell, with a question mark next to them. "It's the same old story, though. Why wait all these years?"

"Maybe he waited because he wanted to distance himself from O'Brian. I still don't understand why he never admitted to me how he had been forced to sell."

"Pride, mate. Who knows, maybe it was such a bad experience he just blocked it out, and you turning up raked up memories he wanted to be left in the past."

"If you ask me, I don't think that he has got the balls to kill O'Brian, but I reckon his sister has."

Shoddy didn't look convinced. "So if she did, why did she let you know what happened when you were quite happily walking away?

Why give herself a motive, and then tell you? It doesn't make sense."

There were a lot of things about O'Brian's murder that didn't make sense to me, and ninety per cent of my head told me that it was Billy that had killed him and that in real life that's just the way murder happened. I was looking for some Agatha Christie type ending and getting nowhere. I wished it could be like Murder on the Orient Express and I could get to a solution that they all did it. O'Brian deserved to die because he was a bad man and ruined people's lives. I didn't need the money, so what the hell was I bothered about? I made a decision. If I hadn't got anything new after talking to Teresa Savage, I would do a final report for Karl Ashford, and tell him I couldn't do anything else. If I were going to do that, I would have to buy a little typewriter, because handwritten reports were not professional enough, especially if you were asking for money. I wondered if I was going to be able to squeeze any more cash out of Karl as a final payment for my services, but wasn't too optimistic.

I called in at the office on my way to see Teresa. There was one message that I hoped was going to be Clair Ashford, but it was Eddie. He said that he was going to be in The Hundred at seven if I wanted to have a drink. I gave Clair another call and left yet another message on her answerphone, then headed off to the pub. I needed a drink before tackling Teresa McCusker.

Eddie was already in the pub when I arrived. I told him the news about Teresa Savage turning out to be the sister of one of O'Brian's old friends from Belfast, and how she had reported an argument between him and Billy Ashford to the police the day he was killed. Eddie agreed with me that it looked like Billy was guilty, especially after I filled him in on what Val Farrell had told me about the beheading of the family dog.

"What are you going to do now, Moggsy? It looks like Billy did it after all."

"I'm going to see Teresa Savage, and then tell Karl Ashford I'm finished. I'm sick of banging my head up against a brick wall, and I reckon I'm not cut out for this private investigator business."

Eddie laughed. "So what are you going to do? I can always get you a job as a bouncer with me if you're that hard-up for something to keep you off the streets."

I finished my pint and whisky chaser and walked with him into the car park. "I Dunno, Eddie. Maybe I will take you up on that offer. Maybe we can start a doorman agency and rent out bouncers to the clubs in Liverpool. I hear you can make good money doing that."

Eddie slapped me on the back and did the punch in the stomach routine again as a goodbye gesture, which I was getting really tired of. "I reckon you should have done what your dad and mum told you to and gone into the family business. Selling second-hand cars is not that bad, and at least you would have had the money to buy yourself something better than the Riley Elf."

"Yeah, can you see me on a used car forecourt selling heaps of junk to gullible old men? I don't have the banter, and I'm too honest."

Eddie looked at my Riley Elf; "You're right mate." He stifled a laugh, "What you're doing now is a much better career choice. Best stick with it eh."

As if on cue, the old Elf chose not to start. It was the cold weather, and I had forgotten to spray damp start onto my leads. Eddie had to push me out of the car park, but even he wasn't strong enough to get the car up to speed for me to do a jump-start in second gear. Thankfully, he was joined by a couple of young lads going into the trendy wine bar across the street. The Elf started with a bang, and black smoke shot out of the exhaust. I kept the revs up down the street while waving my thanks out the window. The little drama with the car had made me late. I hoped that she was going to be in, but if I had known what was in store for me when I arrived, I would have driven home and gone to bed.

CHAPTER SIXTEEN

After the initial problem with the Elf, I made good time as I headed towards the M6 on my way to Legoland. I took a short cut down the B480 to avoid getting caught up in the traffic and arrived outside number eleven with three minutes to spare. It looked promising. The lights were on in the house behind closed curtains, and there was a blue Morris Marina Coupe parked in the drive. I felt the bonnet as I passed. It was cold, so she had obviously been in for a while.

I tapped at the door and waited. Nothing happened, so I tapped a little bit louder, and still, nobody came. I opened the letterbox slightly and could hear the sound of the television. Had she forgotten? I didn't care and had not come all the way to go back without speaking to her.

I opened the letterbox and called her name. I called again and added that we had got an appointment at nine. Inside, there was still just the sound of the television. I moved to the window and tapped it, then tried to peer in through the curtains, but they were closed without any gaps. I realised what this must have seemed like to the neighbours if anyone had been watching, so I went and sat in the car. I had the rather naive hope that she was suddenly going to see sense and come to the door. I looked at my watch. It said twenty past nine. I had been outside her house for twenty minutes. I decided to have one last go before making my way home. I went up the path knocked on the door again a couple of times and waited, before going to the window and tapping it several times.

I moved along the path that led round to the back of the house and came up to the wooden gate that had been locked the last time I had visited. This time my luck was in, and it opened when I tried it. As I went through, I could hear two people arguing. A man and a woman were shouting at the tops of their voices. At first, I thought that the argument was taking place in number eleven, but when I got into the back garden, I realised it was next door. There was a small patio at the back of the house, which led onto an unkempt lawn with overgrown bushes on three sides. Obviously, Teresa was not keen on gardening. The kitchen light was on, and I peered in through the window. There was a door that stood ajar. I could see the television set flickering and could hear it more clearly from this position, as there was a small window that was open above the sink. I shouted her name a few times, then gave it up.

I definitely wasn't going back home without something to show for my night's work. I tried the kitchen door more in hope than anything else and was surprised when it opened. I shut it again quickly, and then on impulse decided to go for it. I opened it a little and shouted Teresa. She must have heard me. I was getting the distinct impression that she was one of these people that go out and leave their television sets on for security, but if she was so obsessed with safety measures, then why leave the kitchen door unlocked?

I entered the kitchen and shouted her name a couple of times, then crossed to the door on the opposite wall. For some strange reason that I can't explain, I knocked and waited. I listened intently and shouted her name again, but she obviously wasn't in. I pushed the door open, intending to have a quick look and go home.

Teresa was lying on the floor of the lounge. She was wearing blue jeans and a white T-Shirt, with a small black hole in the centre that had leaked blood onto the beige carpet. I felt like vomiting and had to take control of myself to curb my desire to run out of the house. Instead, against all my natural instincts, I moved closer and knelt down beside her. The red pageboy hairpiece was half-off her head and revealed her natural hair underneath, which was short and greying brown.

Her eyes were still open, but the beautiful green that had sparkled in anger when I had met her earlier had turned opaque in death. Whoever had killed her had done so face to face, and the force had flung her back onto the floor.

This was the first dead body that I had ever seen and I could feel that I was beginning to panic. I wished Shoddy was with me because, with all of that police training, he would have known what to do. It suddenly struck me that whoever had killed Teresa might still be in the house. I felt the hair standing up at the back of my neck and turned around quickly to look behind me. I half expected the killer to be standing there with a gun. Was it my imagination, or could I hear footsteps on the stairs? I didn't wait to find out but made my exit the same way as I came in.

I knew if the police arrived now, it would not look very good for me and on cue, I could hear sirens in the distance as I walked down the path. As I put the key in the ignition of the Elf, I pleaded with her. "Please don't go dead on me now."

"So who could have done this, Shoddy?"

I had made it back home and was being treated by my friend to a late-night supper of ham sandwiches, with pickle and hot cocoa. What the meal was doing for my stomach was on an equivalent level to what finding Teresa Savage dead had done to my head. Both were in turmoil.

The journey home had been incident-free, but I had used the back roads to avoid the emergency vehicles that were undoubtedly heading to Bill Hayley Close. In my paranoia, I drove around several housing estates and went back onto the M6 for a while to make sure that any potential killer was not following me. Sitting in Shoddy's flat, I shuddered with the thought that whoever had shot Teresa could have shot me. I didn't like the way this case was going and was sure that somebody had taken my registration number, and the police would be arriving any minute.

Shoddy was calm. I guess he must have seen it all before. "Whoever did it must have used some type of silencer if nobody heard anything. Was she still warm when you got there?"

"How the hell do I know? I never touched her."

"So you don't know when she died. It could have been any time during the day."

"Well, not really, because the curtains were drawn, and there were lights on. I suppose it must have been after it got dark, which was around half-past five. It is possible that whoever did it, drew the curtains but I can't see that myself."

Shoddy went over to his easel and wrote 'murdered' at the side of Teresa Savage's name. He drew a couple of lines. One to Billy and the other to a big question mark, which we were using to signify the killer. "This could be the same killer or a different killer with different motives. Let's assume for a minute that Billy killed O'Brian because of his wife having an affair and the argument about drugs. Maybe he came back to kill her because she rang the police and caused all the bother for him. Murder has been committed for less. Think about it, Moggsy. It was a private argument that if she hadn't involved the police, nobody would have known about, and Billy would still be walking around. They probably would not even have interviewed him."

"Billy must have a bloody awful temper to do that. I don't believe it, and who uses guns around here? That's a bit too sophisticated for local villains. Knives and sledgehammers or knuckledusters and baseball bats; but a gun? It just doesn't sound right, plus where do you get a silencer from? That's a bit over the top even for the Ashfords."

Shoddy wrote 'Belfast' on his easel. "I'm still waiting for news about the connection between Tony O'Brian, Paul and Teresa McCusker and Julie Carol. If it is some kind of revenge killing by one of the Para-Military groups out there, then the best bet for us is to pretend it never happened and go back to looking for missing dogs and cats."

"I guess all we can do is wait until tomorrow."

When I got back to my flat, I felt like an idiot, but still spent ten minutes checking that I was alone. My heart was beating double speed when I opened the wardrobe in my bedroom. I pushed the settee against the door, balanced a tray of glasses on top and dug out my trusty baseball bat. Not that it would have been much use against a gun.

I must have laid in bed for a couple of hours before I went to sleep. I was expecting the knock of the police on my door, and even though it never came, when I finally dropped off, I couldn't escape the trauma of what I had seen in eleven Bill Hayley Close. I knew that this was an image that would stay with me forever, and sleep took me back and twisted the images into nightmares. I was so relieved when I eventually woke up at six o'clock the next morning.

CHAPTER SEVENTEEN

My troubled sleep had in a kind of weird way focused my mind on the case, and in that strange room where we all go between being asleep and awake, I got a flash of inspiration. It put a whole new angle on the way we were looking at the two murders and explained a lot of things about why all evidence pointed so blatantly to Billy Ashford. Unfortunately, as anybody who has ever been in that room would confirm, very few ideas make it out into consciousness, and even though I tried, I couldn't get the flash to re-surface. The only thing that I knew was that I had missed something big, which a more logical mind would not have.

I was so convinced that I was missing something that I called in on Shoddy on my way to the office. I declined the full English breakfast that he offered. He tucked into bacon, fried eggs sausage, fried bread, tomatoes and black pudding and I sat in front of the easel with a mug of tea in my hand and a biscuit and stared at the list of names. I wondered how they connected with each other. All roads led to Billy, but maybe that is what they were built for. The guy had been well stitched up if he was innocent, but by who and why? I tried letting my mind go blank and staring at the easel to see if I could pull out what was bothering me from my already overtaxed brain, but it just wasn't happening.

Shoddy came over, eating a piece of fried bread. He looked at me quizzically.

"I think we are missing something, but I don't know what it is. A fact that we are taking for granted has been doctored in some way, and we are just assuming that it's true. If we stopped assuming that, then maybe we would solve the case. Does that make sense, Shoddy?"

"No."

"Great, then it could be I am just going mad." I thought about a better way to explain it. "It's like one of those brain teasers you do where somebody gives you almost all of the facts, but you naturally assume something that isn't true."

Shoddy looked, even more, puzzled now. "How do you mean, Moggs?"

"It's like the case of the man that lives on the 30th floor of a block of flats. Every morning he goes to work and gets in the lift and travels down to the ground floor. When he comes back from work in the evening, he takes the lift to the 10th floor and then walks the rest of the way to his flat. Why?"

"I don't know. Is he afraid of heights?"

"No, he isn't because he lives on the 30th floor."

"Well, he's like you then, Moggsy. He likes to keep fit by running the rest of the way."

"No, he walks the rest of the way."

Shoddy sat and thought for a moment. "The electricity goes off at five o'clock when he comes home?"

"So how does he get up to the 10th floor? It's pure logic, and the reason that you are not getting the answer is that I didn't give you an important fact. Everything is true, but without this fact, you could not reach the correct conclusion."

We sat in silence for a bit and looked at the easel. I was trying to bring to the surface what was bothering me, and I guess Shoddy was attempting to work out why the man only took the lift home to the 10th floor.

"Well, go on then, Moggsy, enlighten me."

"He's a dwarf, and he can't reach the lift buttons."

I planned to be in the office all morning and catch-up on a few bills that needed to be paid. I told Shoddy to telephone me if he got any news from his mate in the Royal Ulster Constabulary. There were two messages on my answerphone. One message was from Eddie, asking if I wanted to meet him for a beer at lunchtime, and a more important one from Clair Ashford, asking me to ring her back. I thought that it was about time for another talk with her, and was pleasantly surprised that she wanted one too. We arranged a mid-morning meeting at my office, which gave me time to get through my work, and saved on petrol.

When she finally arrived, she looked as spectacular in the day, as she had done in the pub at night. From the way she entered my office, I reckoned she loved the fact that even at her age, she could still get men to stare at her. She had her blonde hair down, and it fell over her shoulders in soft, crimped waves. She had a crimson hair band that matched her lipstick, and her deep blue eyes were highlighted to perfection by her eye makeup that even I could see had been expertly applied. She was wearing a black and white pinstripe jacket with a pencil skirt that emphasised her ample figure, and a white blouse that was cut tight to highlight the fact that she had enormous breasts. I was surprised that she was able to sit down in what she was wearing and tried to keep my eyes away from her chest area. I wasn't doing it very successfully, and she gave me that smile that all women have when they know what's on your mind. It's like some secret radar system that they all have that enables your girlfriend from across a crowded room to identify the fact that you are staring at some bimbo's legs. This makes the car journey home after a party like an SS interrogation session.

Clair Ashford didn't look like a woman living in fear that her husband was going down for murder, but what did I know? I had only ever had a couple of girlfriends and gained most of my knowledge about the opposite sex by staring at them from a distance.

She didn't waste any time. "What have you found out, Mr Shannon?"

I gave her the abridged version of events because after all, she wasn't paying me. I left out my dead body encounter and instead honed in on the argument that Billy had with O'Brian the day he was killed. I asked her if she knew anything about it, and she shook her head.

"You understand, Mrs Ashford that this argument is quite damning evidence that there was a motive, and there is a witness (Not anymore) that says he threatened to kill O'Brian, and then a couple of hours later he was dead."

"My Billy didn't have anything to do with Tony's death."

"So you keep telling me, but with all due respect, the facts say otherwise. There was a threat, and he had a motive. He also had the time, and he doesn't have an alibi. He has a police record of violent behaviour, which makes him a dangerous person to mess with." I tried to knock her off balance. "Did he ever hit you, Mrs Ashford?"

She hesitated, and did I see a hint of a blush under all that makeup? "Billy could be a bit physical. Some men are like that, but he always made it up to me. It is just the way he is. But he could never kill somebody the way O'Brian was killed. I read about it in the paper. That was vicious, and Billy isn't vicious, he just had a bit of a temper."

"Weren't you taken to hospital by ambulance on one occasion? That must have been some temper tantrum."

She looked me coolly in the eyes. "You were never married then, Luv?"

I shook my head.

"Yeah, I can see that. You don't look the type. It's give and take in most relationships. Billy used to give it, and I used to take it." She laughed at her joke. "That doesn't mean that we don't love each other, and most of the time, I probably deserved it."

 God, can there really be women like Clair Ashford walking the streets? I changed my approach. "So you still haven't heard anything?"

"He knows where I am, and I know he is going to contact me when it all settles down in his head. That's why you are so important at the moment, Mr Shannon. You're the only one in our corner fighting his case. Everybody else has already convicted him in their heads. You are our only hope."

I felt really bad having to tell her that I also was pretty firmly convinced that Billy was guilty as hell, so I bent the truth a little. "To be perfectly honest, Mrs Ashford. I don't think Karl is happy with what I've done so far, so he is probably not going to pay me anymore."

If I thought that this was going to stop her, I was wrong. She opened up her purse and counted out a substantial amount of twenties and placed them on the desk. "Is that enough to keep you looking for the real killer?"

I began to protest, and she threw some more on the pile. Just then, the phone rang. It was Shoddy. His mate had called, and he wanted me back at the flat right away. He also asked if I would bring fish and chips for our lunch as well. What could I do in the circumstances but accept Clair's offer? I asked her to tell Karl that I was now working for her and not him, and she agreed. I didn't feel guilty about it because after all, me and Karl hadn't got a written contract or anything and he was not the sort to take me to court.

She offered me her hand before she left, and it was surprisingly firm, but somehow a sad gesture. I felt a bit sorry for her. Even though she looked like a high-class hooker, I believed that she had a heart, and would stand by her man no matter what he'd done to her. I was envious of Billy. How could a violent rogue get such a woman, when the closest thing to a meaningful relationship that I had got was with Shoddy?

Thinking about Shoddy, I'd been a bit short with him on the phone, so I rang him back and asked if he wanted his fish and chips in paper, or in a tray to save on the washing up. We agreed to get a carton of sloppy peas, some rather excellent curry sauce and bread and butter as well.

Shoddy was in a buoyant mood when I arrived at his flat. We sat at the table and ate our fish and chips, and he complained about how he had been on the phone half of the morning. He thought that we should invest in a fax machine and I agreed that it would give us a more professional look.

With the small talk over, at last, he pulled out a couple of sheets of A4 paper full of writing on both sides. He sat back in his chair and told me what his Irish friend had said. It was well worth the wait.

Apparently, Paul McCusker was well known to the RUC and the British Security Services in Northern Ireland, as was his sister Teresa. He had started off as a political thug in the Andersonstown district of Belfast. This was a hotbed of violence, with the Falls Road, and the Shankill Road the separation lines between the Catholic and Protestant communities. He used his sister as a honey trap to lure Protestants over the 'peace lines' where he would be waiting with a couple of his mates to give them a good kicking. There was no hard evidence to convict him, as no Protestant that wanted to keep his kneecaps would stand up and admit that he had gone with a Catholic girl for the promise of sex. Teresa had been involved in a more serious incident when she was still a teenager. A British soldier had been lured back by her and tortured before being killed. This was taken more seriously by the RUC and the British Military, but even though McCusker was identified as the instigator, he was untouchable in a court of law due to a lack of evidence.

The only possible solution would have been a quiet execution by a British Agent, but this was not sanctioned for some reason.

The relationship between McCusker and O'Brian started in Primary school, and though O'Brian was a close friend and business associate, he did not have any known links with any political parties or terrorist organisations. The pair also shared a house together from 1967 until O'Brian moved to England.

It was at the beginning of the 1970s when information of a top IRA Hit-Man with the nickname Redbolt came to the attention of the RUC. With a series of high-profile murders under his belt and some bombings and security van robberies, the name of Redbolt and McCusker were identified by an undercover agent named Echo1, to be the same person. He was working for the British Army. Not long after passing on the information, Echo 1 was found in a shop doorway with a bullet in his head. There was no evidence as to the killer's identity though obvious conclusions were drawn.

McCusker and two other men were killed on the Eire, Northern Ireland border on July the 19th 1972 near the Finn Bridge, which separates County Monaghan in the South and Fermanagh in the North. The car was identified as a Datsun Sunny, which was registered to McCusker. Two days later was the infamous Bloody Friday, when in just over 75 minutes the IRA detonated 22 bombs all over Belfast, killing nine people and injuring over 130. The theory of the car bomb was that the three men were either carrying explosives across from Southern Ireland in readiness for the Bloody Friday campaign, and something went wrong, or that it was a roadside bomb assassination by one of the Protestant Paramilitary groups like the UDA or the UDF. Either way, that was the end of McCusker. O'Brian and Teresa left Ireland within days of the killing, though neither was implicated in what had happened. Both had gone off the radar of the security forces. O'Brian turned up in Croxley 12 years ago, and Teresa earlier on this year using her married name.

A couple of interesting facts that Shoddy's mate had dug up were about Teresa McCusker. In 1969, she was admitted to the Royal Victoria Hospital in Andersonstown, after being tarred and feathered and left tied to a lamppost. The punishment was dished out by locals who accused her of sleeping with Protestants. It was believed at the time that she only escaped being kneecapped and crippled for life, because of the respect and fear in the community for her brother. The ringleader of the group that had tarred and feathered his sister was later shot by masked men who broke into his house and executed him in front of his wife and children. Two of the other people involved simply disappeared. Because of the attacks at the time by both sides, the killings and disappearances were put down to Protestant Paramilitary reprisals. It was noted, however, in RUC files that there could be a possible connection with McCusker, who couldn't have been very happy with what had happened to his sister.

Finally, it seems that Teresa did have a preference for Protestants as she got married to Graham Savage, who was Church of England

and an accountant. They lived in Kent until they divorced just before she moved to Merseyside.

After we had finished lunch and washed it down with some strong tea, we went and sat by the easel to talk over how the new information had altered things. Shoddy didn't like the Irish connection and spelt it out in no uncertain terms.

"I don't mind dealing with villains, and I never have done, but terrorist organisations are a different animal. That's why they are called terror groups. Their aim is to put the shits up people by acts of brutality that have no other reason than to send out a warning."

I interrupted him. "But we don't know for sure that it has anything to do with what happened in Ireland. After all, it was over 12 years ago. My bet is that she was killed because she was the only witness to the argument between O'Brian and Billy Ashford. With her out of the way the case falls apart."

"In reality, it doesn't. No matter which way you look, Billy is still number one suspect, and that could be for Teresa Savage's murder as well. He had a motive for both of them, but on the other hand..." He lit up a cigarette and went into his reflective mode.

"On the other hand?"

"Well, on the other hand, Moggsy could it be possible that a link from the past has discovered where Teresa Savage was living and carried out a revenge killing?"

"Revenge for what, though?"

"If she was a honey trap, then there could be plenty of people that may have a grudge, and I don't rule out one of the Protestant Paramilitary Organisations. The Ulster Defence Association for one. Are you telling me that the UDA doesn't have any strong links with Merseyside? She would have been better off staying in Kent because Liverpool is rife with sectarianism violence."

"So what is the link between the two killings?"

"There is a possibility that there isn't a link, but if a link exists, it is shaky. If Billy killed O'Brian, what was his reason for killing Teresa Savage?"

"I don't know. Temper?"

Shoddy ignored me. "If it was some terrorist organisation like the UDA that killed Savage, why did they kill O'Brian? He doesn't have any connections with anything like that. He was a tough, violent, gangster that could be very ruthless in his business dealings, but that's not a good enough motive for a Protestant military group to murder him. Plus, the way it was done is so different. One victim dies in a fire with his head smashed in, and his hands tied behind his back. The other with a bullet through the heart that looks like a professional job. I don't buy that it's the same killer."

When I got out of Shoddy's flat, my head was spinning, and I needed some normal time, with normal people to relax my brain. I headed for The Hundred, drank myself into a stupor and staggered home. I fished out a bottle of very old single malt and sat on the balcony nursing my glass, and savouring the fine old smoky flavour. I was still certain that there was something that I was missing, but it was like waiting for water to come out of your ear when your head had been under the shower for too long. You knew it was there, but it had gone too deep into your eardrum. It took a lot of shaking before it eventually came out. I lay awake that night and gave myself a headache trying to figure out what it was that was bugging me, and by the time I had drifted off to sleep, I had convinced myself that it was just my imagination.

CHAPTER EIGHTEEN

I didn't spend much time in the office the next morning but used Eddie's phone message to meet him in the pub, as an excuse to get to The Hundred at opening time. Eddie was already there when I arrived. He was reading the local newspaper. He passed me the paper for me to have a look. Teresa's death had made a column on the front page though it was not the lead story. There was no mention of a Riley Elf parked outside the house, and whoever had written the story didn't link the fact that she used to work at one of Tony O'Brian's clubs. There was no mention of any private detectives that were wanted for questioning. I had to admit I was relieved.

Eddie was waiting there like a dog with his tongue hanging out, wanting to know what I knew, and I filled him in on the details. When I had finished, he went to the bar and came back with beer and whisky chasers.

"You were lucky that you didn't get there earlier. Otherwise, you might have ended up with a bullet in your head."

I didn't believe in fate, but I realised that the car not starting without a push could have saved my life. "It's a good job that you couldn't push hard enough on your own; otherwise, I might have bumped into the killer. Who do you think did it? Do you think it is linked to O'Brian?"

Eddie shook his head. "I couldn't say, Moggsy, but it certainly seems to be a coincidence. All I can say about the Irish is that they have got themselves a heap of trouble out there in Belfast, and both sides can be ruthless. If it is IRA or the UDA, then maybe it's best that you just leave it. I was only out there for a couple of months, and I was glad to get back in one piece. If Teresa Savage was getting Protestants beaten up and soldiers killed, then she is bound to be on someone's hit list no matter how long ago it was. I got the feeling in Belfast that it's just in their blood to fight, and they would be doing it anyway, even if the Army got out. Some of them got off on the violence."

I got some more drinks and brought back the lunch menu. We ordered a ploughman's each, which at The Hundred consisted of a lump of Welsh Cheese, some pickles, and crusty white bread. I was at a loose end with the case, and the beer and whisky didn't help very much though I welcomed the buzz I was getting.

Eddie picked up on my gloomy mood. "What's next, Moggsy? Are you going to interview the two bookies to see what they know? Or lie low for a while and get drunk on Clair Ashford's money?"

"To be honest, mate, I think I will give her a call tonight and say that I can't carry on anymore. I've reached as far as I can go and seeing that dead body didn't fill me with confidence about the business I'm in. Maybe we should start that agency for doormen."

"You mentioned a fish and chip shop last time you were discussing possible career paths. Will Shoddy be helping you?" It was the drink talking and he knew it, so we settled down and played darts until closing time and I staggered home and dropped like a corpse into my bed.

I was up and out of bed in five minutes, though. It was something that Eddie had said in the pub. It was a crazy idea, but I needed to telephone Julie Carroll. I wished that I had a filing system, which was more orderly because I couldn't remember where I had put her number, or even if she had given it to me. I had the address in Dewsbury though, and I phoned directory enquiries praying that she was not ex-directory. She wasn't.

It took her ages to answer the phone, but to my relief, she eventually picked it up. I chose my words carefully. "Hello is that, Julie Carroll?"

"Speaking," she said cautiously. "Who is this, please?"

"Hello, Julie, it's me, Morris Shannon. Do you remember that I called to see you the other day about Tony O'Brian's death?"

Her voice brightened. "Oh yes, of course, I remember you. How could I forget somebody your size? How are you, Luv?"

"Well, I am very good at the moment, but there is something that you said when I saw you that maybe you could clarify for me."

"Of course, Mr Shannon, what is it?"

"Do you remember when we were speaking about the two boys, you mentioned that Paul McCusker had a violent temper?"

"I do indeed, Luv. He could be an animal when he was roused, and certainly not a gentleman like Tony."

"You also said that it was in the blood. Do you remember?"

"Yes, vaguely."

"What did you mean by, in the blood?"

"Well, you know what they say about redheads, they all have bad tempers: It's in their psychological makeup."

"So was Tony a redhead as well?"

"Oh no, Tony had lovely black hair and blue eyes. He was a real gigolo. He looked like Valentino."

CHAPTER NINETEEN

"It is probably best if you went to the police with this, Moggsy, there is obviously more to this than meets the eye." We were sitting in Shoddy's flat drinking tea and wondering where this new information had taken us. If it was true, and I had no reason to doubt that it wasn't, then Paul McCusker had somehow swapped places with Tony O'Brian and taken his identity. His sister had joined him, and they had both been murdered. Try as I might, I couldn't believe now that this was the work of Billy Ashford; it was too big. I just didn't buy into the idea that it was all about drugs being sold in the Oasis and Kabin clubs. To me, it looked as if it had been a professional hit, and the motive was something that went back to Belfast to the early days of the troubles.

I felt like an idiot for not thinking of it earlier when Julie Carroll had shown me the old picture. It is funny how you just assume things and don't question them. She told me it was Tony O'Brian and Paul McCusker, and there was no reason for me to ask her, which was which. I didn't feel very much like a detective, but Shoddy had gone easy on me and said that it was a mistake that anyone would have made.

Before I went to the police, there was something that I had to do. I had to inform Clair Ashford that it looked as if Billy could be in the clear. Shoddy had already adjusted his easel and linked both deaths to a question mark. He had rubbed Bill's name out.

"How much should I tell the police?"

Shoddy rubbed his chin and thought for a moment. "I don't think that you should mention that you had been in Teresa McCusker's house and seen the body. They may get a bit funny about that. Tell Clair Ashford, then go to the police station and say what you have discovered by talking to Julie Carroll. Say that you have been working for Karl Ashford and that should be enough.

"Talk to Detective Inspector Ives. He is reasonably pleasant, and you can mention my name if you want. I used to be his boss when he was a constable."

"I wonder why, after all these years, they decided to kill them both?"

Shoddy laughed. "You are never going to make a decent detective if you can't work that out. It must have been that television programme that got McCusker noticed. It was the sort of publicity he didn't want, and that was why he got angry. Why he didn't get rid of that red hair smacks of nothing more than arrogance to me, and the ironic part about the whole thing is that by getting angry on TV he must have drawn a lot more attention to himself."

I hadn't thought of that. "If it is a paramilitary operation, what will the police do?"

"Pass it on to the intelligence services, probably, and they will investigate it as best they can. More than likely, they will not get anywhere and file it away. It's just a couple more deaths to add to the list."

There was something a bit depressing about the whole thing, but at least, Billy should be happy. That is unless the police still wanted to press charges to make everything nice and uncomplicated. Of course, there was a chance that the terrorist group had hired Billy, but who would ever believe that?

It was about seven-thirty when I telephoned Clair. I told her that I had some good news, and she invited me around to her house. I couldn't see any point in keeping her in suspense, so I said that I would get there as quickly as I could. I told Shoddy to wait up for me, little realising that I wouldn't make it back that night.

I was being impetuous again. I should have gone around in the morning, having first told the police, but logical thinking has never been one of my strong points, and I was about to suffer for it.

CHAPTER TWENTY

Clair and Billy had a semi-detached out on a new housing estate off the A565, which connects Croxley to Bootle. From Shoddy's flat, it only took me twenty minutes, and when I arrived, I was ushered into the lounge by Clair. She was dressed in a pink tracksuit and matching fluffy slippers. She turned the television down and offered me a drink off a silver tray on the sideboard. I should have refused after the amount I had drunk in the afternoon, but I settled for a whisky, and she poured me a very generous amount into a large glass tumbler. I took a mouthful and rolled it on my tongue, savouring the peaty flavour. It was single malt and expensive. Billy obviously had good taste when it came to his drink.

As always, she got down to business pretty quickly without observing any pleasantries. She took a sip of her gin and tonic. "So you have some good news for me, Mr Shannon."

"I have obtained some information today, which I believe might make the police look elsewhere for the person who killed O'Brian." I told her the story, pretty much as it was, and she listened intensely occasionally nodding but not interrupting me until I had finished.

"You have done well, Mr Shannon. It's amazing what you have found out, but will the police believe you?"

"I don't see any reason why not, and even if there is any doubt, a visit to see Julie Carroll, and a look at the photo that she showed me should be enough. I don't think that there is any doubt that Billy is not guilty and that the McCuskers were murdered as some type of revenge killing because of what they had done in Belfast."

She poured us both another drink, even though I protested, though not very strongly. "What should Billy do now?"

"If you want my opinion, the best thing that he can do is give himself up and let the police sort it out. Just by coming out of hiding will show good-faith and at least he can then give his side of the story; though obviously no mention of the warehouse robbery."

She thought about it for a moment and then got up. "Will you excuse me for a moment, Mr Shannon?" She never waited for a reply, but pushed the bottle of whisky towards me, turned the television up and disappeared into the hall. I resisted another drink and started to watch a news programme about Chinese Triads in Amsterdam. I was getting quite into it when she came back and switched the television off. She sat down, looking solemn.

"I've just been talking to Billy." She saw the look on my face. "I know, I should have told you that I knew where he was, but how did I know that you wouldn't go straight to the police?"

"There is such a thing as client confidentiality," I said, though not sure if that was just for doctors and priests. Anyway, I was a bit annoyed that she hadn't been entirely honest with me. "Does Karl know where he is?"

She shook her head. "Not unless he has told him and lied to me. As far as I know, I am the only one that he gave his address too, but if you can't trust your wife, then who can you trust?"

"Have you known all along?"

"I didn't know until a couple of days ago. Billy has been very secretive and called me from a phone box with the telephone number of the place he is staying. I told him what you said, and he was quite pleased, but not enough to give himself up. He says he will only do that if he speaks to you."

I smiled. "No problem. Give him a call now, and I will tell him what the situation is and what I think he should do."

"No; I don't think you understand. He wants to see you in person; otherwise, he won't give himself up. He says that he wants to look you in the eyes to see if you are lying. Will you come with me?"

I looked at my watch. It was ten o'clock. "Where is he? Is it local?"

"It's not too far, and you can follow me if you want. He has given me directions." She saw the expression on my face, and reached into her handbag "If it's a question of money, Mr Shannon."

I could have done with the money, but the look of desperation on her face was enough. I only hoped that I could persuade her husband to walk into a police station. "Where is he hiding?"

"It's just up the motorway, in Anglesey." She added, "At least let me fill your tank up before we go."

CHAPTER TWENTY-ONE

It was a glorious night for a drive, but an even better one to be in bed with a cup of hot chocolate and some biscuits or curled up on the settee with a blanket watching a film. It was one of those winter nights that you often get on Merseyside, with a cloudless sky filled with stars and a half-moon. Some people get a buzz out of nights like these and go on about ambience, but for me, it was something I could have done without. I wished that I had brought a thicker coat with me and that the heater in the Elf worked better. In fact, it didn't work at all,

I was following behind Clair's Ford Capri, and hoping that the Elf was going to make it to Anglesey and back without letting me down. I was surprised that she wanted me to follow her rather than go together, but she insisted. Her argument was that it was the best for me, as I could leave when I had finished. I assumed by this that she was going to stay the night.

We made good time getting out of Merseyside. Clair chose to go under the river using the Birkenhead tunnel and then pass through Bebington and Ellesmere Port en route to the A55, which is the coast road into North Wales. By the time we got to Conway, I had no feeling in my feet, and as we crossed the suspension bridge over the Menai Straights that separated the island of Anglesey from the civilised world, my eyes were closing.

I had never been to Anglesey before, and from what I could see of it, I had not missed much. Without the lights of the Capri guiding my way, I would have been lost. I got a distinct impression that either she was an ex-girl guide and had taken her map reading badges or she had been here before. When she left the A55 and took the B4545, I saw a sign for a place called Trearddur Bay that was two miles away. I hoped that this was our final destination.

The Capri headed on a small road beside a beach that glistened in the winter moonlight. The tide was out, and I could see that we were moving around a little bay, with rocks on either side. The place was deserted, and none of the houses that we passed had lights on, which I suppose was not surprising seeing as it was after midnight.

She turned into a small path that ran at 90 degrees to the beach, which most people would have missed, as there was no sign that I could see. I was now convinced that Clair had been here before. The path we were on was not doing my suspension any good, but the bumps woke me up. At the top, we came to a white wooden gate marked Private. It was closed, and Clair got out of her car and opened it. She walked over to me, and I wound the window down.

"Not far now," she said and pointed vaguely up to the road after the open gate, which at least had tarmac. She saw that I was shivering. "Don't worry, we will be in the warm soon. Just another two minutes."

I followed her through the gate and waited while she closed it after us. The road wound up a steep hill for about half a mile then dropped away to reveal a small whitewashed cottage with woods on three sides. It reminded me of the sort of place the three bears would have lived when Goldilocks stole their porridge, and if I were choosing a place to hide, I would have chosen this one. I pulled up beside the Capri and got out, swinging my arms to get some feeling back in them and stamping my feet. I followed Clair up the path and stood behind her while she knocked on the door. I said amicably enough "Are you sure that you have never been here before because you found it very well?"

She turned around and smiled, and then I felt my head explode. I staggered around for a couple of seconds and tried to grab onto her. She stepped back, and I fell onto the floor and blacked-out.

I woke up, and the first thing that I realised was that I was strapped very securely to a chair. Though I could move my hands, I couldn't move my body even an inch. I opened my eyes slowly and took in the scene.

I was sitting in the middle of a fairly large room facing the front door, which is what Clair had presumably knocked before someone had hit me. At the side of the door was a window that had the curtains drawn, and to the left was a dining table where Clair was sitting with her back to me smoking a cigarette. There was an old-fashioned three-piece suit around a black and white television on a mahogany table that was switched off. The room wasn't cold, so I assumed there must be some form of central heating because I couldn't see any fire.

I heard footsteps approaching from behind, and an Irish voice that I didn't recognise said "You're awake at last. Clair was convinced that the blow had killed you, but I knew you were made of sterner stuff, Mr Shannon. How are you feeling?"

The man came around the chair and stood in front of me, smiling. He had short red hair and was holding a glass of what looked like brandy. It was McCusker; the bastard wasn't dead after all. Clair came up and stood beside him, and he put his arm around her and kissed her gently on the cheek. He repeated the question to me about how I was feeling.

"How would you expect me to feel, I have just been knocked out and am sitting tied to a chair, with a head that feels like it's going to burst any moment."

"I'd give you an aspirin willingly, Mr Shannon, but I don't think you will be needing one where you are going. I can assure you that this is nothing personal, but you are just a loose end that I need to tidy up before leaving."

I didn't like the sound of this and tried to keep the panic out of my voice when I spoke. "You know, of course, that I have informed the police, and they are probably on their way as we speak."

That didn't even get an answer from him; he just laughed, wagged his finger in my direction and disappeared behind me again. I didn't like him being behind me where I couldn't see what he was doing or about to do. There was the sound of his footsteps going upstairs, and I could hear him walking about on the floor above. That just left Clair and me and what I can only describe as a hugely embarrassed silence. I knew that she was going to start up a justification rant, and she didn't let me down.

"I know what you are thinking, Shannon."

I bet she didn't, but up there in my thoughts was why people always dropped the Mr when they wanted to make me feel bad?"

She lit another cigarette and continued. "Billy was a monster to live with, but I put up with it for years. I even put up with losing our baby, after he knocked me down the stairs in a rage one night. I didn't leave him either when the hospital told me that I couldn't have another one. But do you know what I couldn't put up with, and what finally made me want to kill him?"

I shook my head. I didn't have a clue and couldn't give a damn either.

"I couldn't put up with the fact that one of his girlfriends got pregnant, and he became a dad. I only found out by accident, when I found a fucking pushchair folded up in the boot of his car. If anyone deserved to die, it was Billy. He murdered my baby, so it was justice."

I looked into her eyes. She was totally mad. How I had not seen it before, I put it down to the fact that my detecting skills were minimal. "So what are you going to do now, Clair? You know they will catch you; they always do. Don't you think a divorce would have been less drastic?"

"Paul agrees with me that Billy didn't deserve to live. I watched him do it, with a mallet. The only pity was that he was dead before he was burned. You can't imagine the hell that man put me through, in fact, only Paul understands."

"You know about McCusker's past, don't you? Compared to him, Billy was Mary Poppins."

"Now that's a bit hard, don't you think, Mr Shannon?" McCusker was back. "And besides, Clair is a good Catholic girl, and she understands the circumstances. We are fighting a war in Ulster, and in a war, you do what you need to do to win."

"Does that mean letting one of your best friends get blown up so you can take his identity?"

He went over to the table, took a pistol out of the drawer and checked that it was loaded. I needed to engage him in conversation and get him distracted. "How come you chose Tony O'Brian to take your place? Did you have an argument or something and that was his payback?"

It wasn't working. He ignored me and walked behind my chair with the gun. Clair went and sat by the table and looked at the wall. I closed my eyes and waited for the inevitable. The only thing that came into my head at that exact moment was that I hoped Shoddy was not still waiting up for me.

The blast of the gun was deafening in the confined space. I slumped forward in the chair, then opened my eyes as I realised that I had not felt any pain, and it was only a reflex action.

Clair was lying on the floor by the table, and if it wasn't for the hole in her neck that was beginning to ooze blood, she looked like she was sleeping.

McCusker stood in front of me, holding the pistol casually by his side. "Don't worry; she didn't feel anything." He looked at his watch. "And neither will you. By the time they find the both of you, I will be well on my way to another life, with another identity in a country that doesn't have an extradition treaty with Britain."

It's funny, but McCusker made death by shooting sound almost pleasant. As he was talking to me, I noticed that the door handle was turning ever so slightly. I looked him in the eyes and spoke louder in an attempt to hide any noise. "Why after all this time did you decide to run, McCusker?"

"He looked at his watch again. " I'm sorry, my friend, but time is up for you. I'm going to make it as quick and painless as I can. I wish that there was another way, but like I said before I can't leave any loose ends."

Somebody coughed slightly, and McCusker turned his head in the direction of the sound. Standing by the door, was a man in a green balaclava that covered all of his face except for his eyes. He had a gun with a silencer on it, which he fired. McCusker fell against my chair and slid down onto the floor. The masked gunman walked over to Clair, checked she was dead, and then walked over to McCusker and rolled his body over with his foot. He must have still been breathing because he shot him again twice through the heart.

The gunman turned towards me but lowered his gun. He stood in front of me for what seemed like a long time but must have been just a few seconds. It was as if he was making up his mind what to do. Finally, he turned around and walked out through the door, closing it behind him.

CHAPTER TWENTY-TWO

The clock on the wall in the cottage said 4:20 when the masked gunman left. The least he could have done was untie me. As it was, I was stuck in a room with two dead bodies in a cottage in the middle of nowhere, with zero chance of escaping. It had not been one of my better days so far, and now that the possibility of getting shot in the head had diminished, I had a new problem to solve, or I would be discovered sometime in the future having died of malnutrition or boredom.

For all my efforts to reach the door while still attached to the chair, all that I succeeded in doing was to fall on Paul McCusker. His empty eyes and body in the early stages of rigour-mortis made me roll away pretty quickly.

It was eight o'clock when the door eventually opened, and in strode Eddie dressed in a grey anorak, waterproof trousers, and walking boots. "Morning, Moggsy," he said casually. "Sorry I'm a bit late, but we've had a busy night." He looked at the two dead bodies. "Clair and McCusker?"

I nodded my head. "Can you get me out of this chair, Eddie?" I shouted on the edge of hysteria.

"Will do, mate, then we can have a nice cup of tea and a chat."

As Eddie was releasing me from what turned out to be a very complicated padlock, four men appeared with stretchers and carried out the two bodies. They were dressed in white overalls and didn't utter one word while they were in the room. Another one dressed in a suit came into the room, disappeared through the door behind me. He came back with two cups of coffee, just as Eddie opened the lock and set me free. He was obviously an undercover waiter.

I sat down at the table, and Eddie sat across from me and played with his spoon while I drank my coffee. He looked slightly embarrassed, but I wasn't going to make it easier for him by speaking first. "I can give you most of the answers, Moggsy, but some I don't even know myself."

"The one I want to be answered first is how did you find me out here?"

"I bugged the Elf, so I knew where you were at all times. I followed you here last night, but we were waiting for things to develop before I could come in to get you out."

"We?

"I work for a special undercover branch of the military. It's all hush-hush. I was put into the Oasis to observe and report back what the situation was with McCusker, but I messed up a little bit, and then you came in, Moggsy, and saved the day."

"You've lost me. What's been going on here?"

"In brief, Moggsy. Paul McCusker was an IRA operative whose codename was Redbolt. He was a top man and carried out executions, armed robberies, and kidnappings. After what happened to his sister, Teresa, McCusker was so angry that he walked into a British Army barracks in the middle of the night and said that he wanted to become a double agent. And that is what happened. For several years he worked for us and fed us a fair bit of information. But because the security out in Ulster is leaky, he was only known to a few men at the top of the ladder. He was one of our best-kept secrets. His working name for us was Redace, and even the RUC didn't know that he existed. They just knew him as an IRA operative. I don't have the details of why, but for some reason, McCusker thought that his cover had been blown, and he sent in a specially coded message to say so, using his name Redace. He thought that he was going to be killed. The next thing that the Special Forces knew was that he had been blown up on the border and that he was dead.

Only a few people at the top knew what had happened, and that it was O'Brian who was driving McCusker's Datsun. Coincidence or planned? I don't know, and now that he is dead, we will never find out. Anyway, those people at the top knew that he was using O'Brian's identity, and let it go. They also knew that before he had faked his death, he had been stashing away money from various armed robberies in Northern Ireland that should have been handed over to his IRA bosses.

It was not long ago, when McCusker's old coordinator got a message from Redace, saying that he thought his cover was blown in

Merseyside and that he needed to get out fast. I was sent in to keep an eye on the situation and report anything strange. I wasn't even told that Teresa Savage was his sister. Apparently, it was the television program that had spooked him, and he was worried that somebody would spot him and also go for her.

As it was, I never saw it coming. McCusker stopped drugs being sold in his clubs and caused a big argument with the Ashfords, which Teresa McCusker reported to the police on the day before his alleged death. The night that McCusker disappeared, I was working on the door at the Oasis and was as surprised as anybody else that Billy's name was mentioned in connection with the murder. I didn't even know that he had left the club on the night that he died, and my controller wasn't too pleased with what had happened. And then, you stepped in, Moggsy, and in your own way got to the bottom of it."

"I don't get it; I was about to give up on the case, and Clair Ashford paid me money to carry on. Why would she do that, if she had so much to hide?"

"You did too good a job, Moggsy, and McCusker was just covering all the options. By getting Clair to pay you, it meant that if you got near the truth, then you would report it to her before going to the police, and you have to be honest; it worked."

"But I was not going to carry on. I told her."

"Why do you think McCusker stayed alive for so long, Moggsy? He covered every eventuality, no matter how slight. It was just possible that more information would come up. In fact, that's what happened, and what did you do?"

I could see his point. "Yeah, okay, I went straight to tell Clair about it." I felt like I had been an idiot and changed the subject. "So you're a secret agent, Eddie?"

"More like an undercover military copper that blends into the background and listens on the streets to what's going on. You would be surprised at what is happening around you that is linked to crime or terrorism that you don't know about. The McCusker job was a step-up from my usual stuff, and after the mess I made, it looks like I'm back to information gathering." He added under his breath "On less money too."

"When did you put a bug on my car?"

"I did that a couple of days after we first met in the Oasis. I also messed up your flat a bit. Sorry about that, but I was trying to scare you into backing off, as I didn't want you digging up anything. In the end, my controller said that I should bug your car and just leave you to it as he didn't think you would get anywhere."

"You set me up at the pub, to get beaten up by Deggsy and his mates as well didn't you? Were you still trying to scare me off?"

"It apparently didn't work, did it? It was for your own good. I was trying to keep you out of harm's way, Moggsy, because these are dangerous people, but you just kept getting closer and closer to the truth."

"Where were you when that masked gunman came in and shot McCusker?

"Outside in the woods. We couldn't come in and rescue you as I was told very clearly that we had to wait and then follow the gunman after he shot McCusker. We knew that he was coming, just didn't know when."

"So you knew that McCusker was going to be shot, and you let it happen. I thought that he worked for you. What if the gunman had shot me as well?"

Eddie started playing with his spoon again. "It all turned out alright in the end, Moggs."

"Yeah but no thanks to you, Eddie."

"There is no black and white here I'm afraid, Moggsy. No good guys and bad guys. It's a bloody mess, and we are all different shades of grey. I'm sorry that you got pulled in."

"Who was that gunman?"

"The same one who shot Teresa McCusker possibly, at the moment I can't say. We will track him and find out who his associates are, then track them. That's the way it works. Information gathering. These people are better left alive so they can lead you around the cell that they are working in. It's like pulling up weeds. You need to dig and get all of the roots; otherwise, you are wasting your time."

I looked down, and there were specks of blood on the floor. "Where does Clair Ashford fit into all of this?"

Eddie shrugged. "Paul McCusker used people. She was just a victim. He must have picked up on her hatred of Billy during the couple of years they were seeing each other and turned it to his advantage. That was a particular skill of his, and that is why he was so dangerous. I reckon it was her that phoned the local paper to tell them about the affair, to put Billy further in the shit."

I shook my head. "I can't understand the mentality of McCusker."

"That's not such a bad thing, Moggsy, because if you did understand him, then you would be as bad as him."

"So who did the police chase from Billy's house on the morning of the murder, if he was already dead?"

"Probably McCusker dressed up in his clothes."

We finished our coffee and walked outside. A dark blue Citroen was waiting with the engine running, with three men inside. For some reason, Eddie shook my hand before driving off but thankfully didn't do the playful punches to my stomach routine. He said that he would be in touch, though I couldn't understand for what reason.

I climbed into the Riley Elf looking forward to getting back to Merseyside and normality. I turned the key and nothing. The cold must have drained the battery. I sighed, locked her up, and started the walk into the village, hoping that there was a garage and that it would be open.

EPILOGUE

I didn't make it home until early evening, but even though I was shattered, I had to sit down and share my adventures with Shoddy. He looked as if he hadn't slept either.

The next few days felt a bit strange not having a case to work on, and I settled into a routine of pub, afternoon television, pub, and bed. I checked my answer phone messages daily in the hope of another client, but nobody wanted to hire me. I decided to put an advert in the local newspaper, and Shoddy, and I sat up until the early hours writing it.

I never heard from Karl Ashford again, probably because he got ten years for robbing the Warehouse in Bootle.

The more I thought about it, the less sure I was that the masked gunman was an Irish terrorist. He could have been anyone. I remember that he was big and that he didn't say anything, so was it possible that it was Eddie, taking care of 'loose ends' for the British Security Forces? I convinced myself that this was as likely a scenario as any. However, there was not much chance that I would ever find out and even if I did what difference would it make? Both the IRA and the Secret Service were as bad as each other.

Eddie did turn up as promised and asked me if I wanted to do some more work for him. When I asked what type of work it was, he said that it just involved a little bit of surveillance and information gathering. I told him that I would think it over.

And I still am.

THE END

Thank you for reading the Penny Detective. If you enjoyed it, pass it on and tell some of your friends.

Visit my author page here: Visit Amazon's John Tallon Jones Page Click FOLLOW, and you will get up-to-date information on all future releases.

If you want to contact me with any comments, ideas or thoughts about the book, or just for a chat, look me up on:

Facebook: https://www.facebook.com/john.t.jones.52

Twitter: https://twitter.com/john151253.

Email me at john151253@gmail.com to go on my mailing list for information about new books coming out. I never divulge any information to a third party.

I always reply and am always very happy to hear from you.

Other books in the Penny Detective Series are:

1. The Penny Detective

2. The Italian Affair

3. An Evening with Max Climax

4. The Shoestring Effect

5. Chinese Whispers

6. Murder at Bewley Manor

7. Dead Man Walking

8. The Hangman Mystery

9. Flawed

10. The Black Rose Murders

11 The Elephant Room

12 A Simple Case of Murder

13 Murder at Woodley Grange

Before you go, here is a little bit of another book in the Penny Detective series.

THE ITALIAN AFFAIR

Winter 1986

CHAPTER ONE

One of the curious things about being a private detective is the reaction you get from strangers when you tell them what job you do. I don't mean people that you meet in the course of a case; it's the ones you get talking to in the pub, or at a party, that can get up your nose and destroy your day, or if you're not working very much, your month. The conversation always goes the same way. They ask you what you do for a living. You answer, and they either laugh and say "You're kidding" and change the subject or laugh and mention some famous detective like Columbo, Inspector Clouseau or Perry Mason. I then have to explain is not a detective but a bloody lawyer. I'm grateful for the fact that I hardly ever get invited to parties these days anyway, and the people I talk to in my local pub, are usually limited to my best mate Shoddy, or occasionally the landlord Bill.

My name is Morris Shannon, but most people I know call me Moggsy. I never had aspirations when I was young about being a private detective or doing anything remotely connected with police work. I sort of drifted into the idea mainly because I saw a Course advertised in the Daily Mirror that I could do from home and ticked all of the boxes I was looking for at the time. It meant I was working for myself, was not tied to a desk, and would piss off my mum and dad good style because they wanted me to go into the family business.

It could have been the shock of my new profession that finally pushed dad over the edge, and made him sell his Second-Hand Car business, retire and move with my mum to Sunny Spain. Thankfully that was after mum persuaded him to set up a fund that gave me a small monthly income, which meant I wasn't going to become destitute, and end up living on the streets…again.

The old man doesn't need the money as he is a multi-millionaire, but he didn't get to be that rich by throwing it away. What little I get pays the rent on my one-bedroom council flat, and my office, which is above a betting shop on the High Street in Croxley Greater Merseyside.

I'm 30 years of age and have been a private investigator for two years, but got my first big case a couple of months ago, which almost got me killed. The near-death experience rather than putting me off, in a way made me more determined to try and make a living out of a profession that can give you one hell of a buzz. You are never quite sure what you are going to get involved in when a client comes into your office and sits down in the chair opposite you. The fact that most people put my line of work in the same bracket as lion tamer, cowboy or tree surgeon is just a side-issue I've grown to live with.

It had been a slow Monday morning, and I was just making a cup of tea, smelling the milk to see if it was off, and considering whether it was worth coming in after lunch, or going to the pub when there was a tap on the door. I opened it half expecting it to be another one of the door-to-door insurance salesmen that keep pestering me but was surprised to see a woman standing behind it just starting to knock again. We both laughed as people do as she stopped her fist connecting with my chest instead of the door panel.

"You must be, Morris Shannon," she said, looking up at me and smiling.

"Yes, I suppose I must be," I replied, rather flippantly considering this was a potential client, and I needed the money for a new set of front tyres for my car. I moved to one side, and she walked in. Once inside the office, we shook hands clumsily, laughed again, and she sat down at my desk and waited for me to join her.

I offered her a cup of tea, but she refused, and I guessed she was probably more into freshly percolated coffee than Yorkshire teabags and sour milk. She was in her mid-thirties and smartly dressed wearing an expensive knee-length black coat with a fur collar and black boots. She had legs that seemed to carry on forever, long straight black hair, with dark, sensuous eyes and from what little I had heard, spoke with a high-class London accent that had a hint of something foreign. She definitely liked the colour black, and I wondered what the rest of her wardrobe looked like, and if I would be getting the chance to see it.

I finished off making my tea, deciding for health reasons to leave out the milk and sat down behind my desk. "So what can I do to help you, Mrs....?"

She smiled and did I detect her flirting at me with her eyes, or was I just lusting? "Call me Katarina, Mr Shannon, my name is Katarina Falcone, and that's Miss."

"Is that a Spanish name or French?" I wasn't particularly interested, but you have to ask.

She smiled and did that flirty thing with her eyes again. "Italian."

"Okay, Katarina, what can I do for you?"

"Well, I hope that you will be able to help me find my brother." She went inside a little black leather shoulder bag that she had on her lap and pushed a piece of paper towards me with some writing on it. "This is his address if you want to write it down. His name is Paulo Falcone."

I was a bit confused by this but wrote the address down on my desk notepad. It was on the Beech Hill Estate on the outskirts of Croxley, which had a pretty bad reputation for just about everything. "So how come he is missing, and how long has it been since you last saw him?"

"I think that I'd better explain the situation, Mr Shannon, it's a bit complicated."

I leaned back in my chair and took a sip of my tea. "Okay, Katarina, in your own time, tell me all about it."

"I live in London, and so did Paulo, but he moved up here about a year ago, and I haven't seen him during this time."

"Did you live together?" I asked

"No, we both had our own apartments, and when he moved up here, he never wrote to me, but he always used to phone on a Sunday until a couple of weeks ago when he stopped."

"He could have gone on holiday, or just been too busy. Do you have his telephone number?"

"I do, but it just keeps ringing. The thing is, Mr Shannon, I need to get in touch as a matter of urgency because our grandmother is seriously ill in hospital in Italy. She has been asking for Paulo, so it's critical that you find him and tell him to come home so that we can fly out."

"So have you been to his house?"

"Yes, that was the first thing that I did when I arrived here last night. I spoke to his landlord, and he said that he didn't live there anymore and that he hadn't left any forwarding address. I need to find him, Mr Shannon. Do you think you can help?"

"Have you tried the police, hospitals anything like that?"

"Why, do you think something has happened to him?"

"I can't say without further information, but if you say that it's not like him to just disappear, then maybe he has had an accident or something, so it's worth taking a look at."

"Could you do this for me, Mr Shannon? I have to go back to London this afternoon, and I wouldn't know how to start looking."

"Are you sure that you don't want to ask the police at least? They have a lot of resources and might be able to help quicker if it's a matter of urgency and your grandmother is asking to see him." Here I was trying to talk her out of hiring me. Those new wheels for my car began to fade in front of my eyes.

Katarina did the trick of opening her eyes very wide for a split second, again and smiled. "I'm sure that it's something that doesn't need the police at this stage. Knowing my brother, he could have moved in with a girlfriend, and just forgotten to phone."

"Has he done this sort of thing before?"

"Well, no, Mr Shannon, but he can be a bit scatty. What's the problem, I thought that this was the kind of work that you type of people did." Her attitude had suddenly gone a little bit abrasive, and I could see by her body language that she was not happy with my answers. This was a lady that was used to getting what she wanted, and at this moment in time, she wanted a type of person like me, so who was I to argue.

I told her my daily rate, and she didn't flinch but went into her bag again, took out her purse and counted out the notes from a huge roll. She handed me the cash and put the rest back in her purse. What she had given me had hardly made a dent, and I wished I had asked for more. "If I give you three weeks, then if you find him sooner, you can give me the rest back. Is that okay?"

For me, that certainly was okay, and I could hardly stop myself punching the air with happiness. No more remoulds for the car, this time, I was going to get Michelins.

"I'll see what I can do, Miss Falcone, and I'm sure that I can turn up something. Have you got a picture of your brother?"

She reached into her bag again, brought out a small passport size picture and handed it to me. He certainly shared the family dark-featured characteristics though he had short black curly hair rather than long and straight like his sister. He was a good-looking bastard, and I estimated he was in his mid-twenties. "When was this taken?" I asked

"That was maybe five years ago." She took the picture back from me and looked at it carefully. I could see her bottom lip begin to quiver, but she controlled it well, took out a paper handkerchief from her bag and wiped her eyes. "I'm sorry, Mr Shannon, what with my Gran and now Paulo doing a vanishing trick."

I always get embarrassed around distressed women, especially ones I don't know very well. "Do you want a drink of water?"

She smiled, shook her head and handed me the photo back. "He was 24 when that picture was taken, so that would make him 29 now. Is there any more information that you want to know?"

"Have you got his work address? What did he do for a living?"

She shook her head. "I know that he was working locally as a van driver, for some firm selling car parts called.......Garret or Galway. It was something beginning with a G and Scottish sounding, but more than this I can't tell you. I should have paid more attention; I know he told me. Is this going to be a problem, Mr Shannon?"

"I think I will be able to find out the company; there aren't that many in Croxley." I wrote down Garret and Galway in my notebook.

"Is there any other information that you want, Mr Shannon?"

"No, I think that is all I need, for now, I'll write you out a receipt for the money, and if you could fill this in for me." I gave her my terms and conditions attached to a form where she could write her personal details. She filled these in using a very expensive looking fountain-pen that she produced from her bag, and passed them back.

I told her I would ring her as soon as I had made some progress and gave her one of my cards. We shook hands again, and I showed her out. I watched her through the office window as she walked away; standing a little back just in case she turned around. That was one hell of a beautiful woman, and the smell of her perfume, I knew, would be in the room for days. I shut the window quickly so it wouldn't drift out; picked up the money she had left and went to the pub.

CHAPTER TWO

Second-home to me is a pub called the The Old One Hundred, which is just a drunken stagger away from my flat. Far from being fashionable, The Hundred is no more than a serious drinker's bolt-hole, and the aggressive vibe you can feel when you walk into the place is enough to keep away the trendies and students, who tend to congregate across the road in the new wine bar or risk the bus into Liverpool.

The Hundred is crying out for a lick of paint and some decent furniture, but like the people that use it, there is a feel about the place that is somehow genuine and not full of the crap you get in a lot of city pubs these days. I love the pub, as does my best mate and partner Shoddy, who I found sitting in one of the old green leather armchairs in the Snug when I strolled in.

Without Shoddy's help, I think that it is fair to say that my detective days would be numbered, as I haven't got the brain or the patience for the boring sifting through files and gathering information that makes up 90 per cent of the job. He had a pint of Bitter in front of him was reading a magazine intensely, and fitted into the ambience of the pub perfectly. People that didn't know him would probably write him off as nothing more than a bum, and I suppose that he was to look at. He had a derelict face, tobacco-stained fingers and an unhealthy aura that like The Hundred had seen better days. He looked like he belonged sleeping rough in a shop doorway, but without a doubt, Shoddy had one of the finest brains of anyone I have ever met.

To think that when I had first been introduced to him, he was a senior officer in the Merseyside Police Force right now beggars belief. He was destined for the top with a bullet, but an addiction to heroin and alcohol destroyed all that, and something that he never talks about was enough to push him over the edge and make him try to kill himself using Paraquat. He was pensioned-off and spends most of his time these days drinking, to forget whatever it was in the past that tipped the balance in his head. If I ever ask him as I sometimes do, what he is trying to forget, he always laughs and says that he can't remember so the drink must be working.

One of his major assets, however, is that there are many serving officers on Merseyside, who haven't forgotten what a sharp mind he has, and he still has more low-life contacts in the Croxley area than half of the force put together. In short, he is my eyes, ears, and brain and when sober is indispensable.

I bought myself a pint with a whisky chaser and sat down in my favourite chair next to him. He didn't look up. "That must be a pretty good read, Shod; you've hardly touched your drink."

"It's my third, but I was going slow and waiting for you because I don't have any money left."

I got the hint and headed for the bar. When I came back, he was draining his glass and took the one I had just bought with a hungry look on his face. "Do you know, Moggsy that they have started doing things on computers that link them up to each other using phone lines and that in 30 years we could see computers linked all over the world. Imagine the advantages of something like that."

"Have you been on the Wacky-Backy again, Shoddy?"

"No, Moggs it's all here in this magazine, in the future there ain't gonna be any paper or books, because it's all going to be done on computers, so small that they can fit in your pocket."

"You'll be telling me next that we're all going to have one. Leave it out, mate; I can't see it happening in our lifetime or cop cars that fly I'm afraid. But anyway I've got a job for us."

Shoddy brightened. "Anything interesting?"

"Not really, but I need your help to trace a lad who has gone missing."

The great thing about Shoddy is that he worked for tobacco and beer, but I couldn't be too generous and give it him all at once because like a dog eating its food, he didn't have the mental capacity to know when to stop. To keep him running smoothly, I needed to give him just enough money for the right amount of alcohol and smokes to keep him alert. If he had too much in one go, he passed through the stage of usefulness and carried on drinking until he was unconscious. It sounds strange, I know, but I'm used to it now, and I think he understands.

I filled him in on the details and left him to think it over while I got the beer in. We ended up buying a bag of fish and chips for a late lunch from the Chippie on the corner and staggering back to his flat, which was conveniently next door to mine, in a high-rise building that had been condemned as unsafe for human inhabitation twenty years ago.

Shoddy's place was a replica of mine, only a mirror image so that where my kitchen was on the right of the hall when you came through the front door, his was on the left. I have to admit that it was kept a lot tidier than mine, but I put that down to the fact that he had nothing else to do all day except get wasted and clean. While I sat on the settee and digested my haddock and chips, Shoddy made us both a cup of tea. He brought mine over and relaxed into his old armchair that was so overused it had a permanent indent of his backside. He rolled a cigarette while we mulled over what course of action we needed to take with the Paulo Falcone disappearance.

"I reckon that it shouldn't be that difficult to trace him, what do you think, Shod?"

"Looks simple on the surface, but I wonder why she came to you rather than let the police handle it. With all due respects, they have more resources at their disposal than you and me."

"So shall I ring her up and insist that she takes the money back?" I joked.

He ignored this remark, lit his rolly and became one with the chair. "What's your plan of action about the landlord?"

"I was thinking of going after I finished my tea and getting that out of the way."

"Steady on, Moggsy, you don't want to finish this in a couple of days and have to give her the money back."

I could see his logic, but thought that I was probably going to find out where he had moved to through his work. "I'll drive up to Beech Hill and see what I can find out. You can check out the places that deliver car parts in the area that sound like Garret or Galway as a start."

"I hope you're giving me a phone allowance on this one, Moggsy; there's gonna be loads listed."

That idea was too ridiculous to answer. "If we can't find out anything from these two leads, then we can start looking around the hospitals. What else can we do to trace him if the worse comes to the worse?"

Shoddy looked at me with despair in his eyes. "Didn't they teach you anything on that bloody course you went on?

I shrugged; "You know me, not very good at reading. I've still got all of the books they gave me in the Wardrobe mostly unopened; you can have em if you like."

"I suggest you read them sometimes if you want to become a real detective."

I suppressed the need to laugh and just nodded my head solemnly in agreement. I could feel a lecture brewing-up. "So go on then, how do you do it; you're the professional?"

"Well, after looking at hospitals, you can look at police records to see if he has been arrested or if he has got any previous. You can check out any known criminal associates at this point and contact them. You need to look on the council housing list, or private housing associations, electoral role, DVLC in Swansea, check if he's married and if so talk to his wife or ex-wife; and that's just for starters. There're lots of ways to trace somebody, but it's not a quick process, and you need patience."

"I bet you wish you lived in that world you described where we could all link-up our computers and find the information that way." I finished my tea and got up. "Time to go to work; I'll see you if I can get in and out of Beech Hill without getting mugged or robbed. Have fun with the phoning."

Printed in Great Britain
by Amazon